"Blaze?"

Blaze blinked agains[...] his heart pinching tight. "Maisy?"

Maisy Daniels had torn into his life late last year like a bullet, ripping past all his walls and pretenses.

Blaze flew onto the porch, drawn by shock and the heartbreak in her voice. She was huddled in the corner, arms curled around herself and thick red hair hanging wet and dark against her cheeks. "What happened? What are you doing here?" He scanned the empty space near his truck for signs of another vehicle he'd somehow missed. Sudden fear clenched his heart and lungs. "Where are the marshals?"

"Dead, I think," Maisy whispered, rolling pleading, tear-filled eyes to meet his. "I didn't know where else to go."

He reached for her, gut wrenching. "Let's get you inside. You're soaked, probably frozen and..." His words were lost as she stretched onto her feet, and her distended silhouette registered in his addled mind. "Pregnant?"

PROTECTING
HIS WITNESS

—

JULIE ANNE LINDSEY

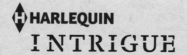
HARLEQUIN
INTRIGUE

This book is dedicated to my Private Eyes,
you know who you are, and I can't thank you enough.

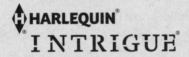

Recycling programs
for this product may
not exist in your area.

ISBN-13: 978-1-335-28460-0

Protecting His Witness

Copyright © 2021 by Julie Anne Lindsey

All rights reserved. No part of this book may be used or reproduced in
any manner whatsoever without written permission except in the case of
brief quotations embodied in critical articles and reviews.

This is a work of fiction. Names, characters, places and incidents
are either the product of the author's imagination or are used fictitiously.
Any resemblance to actual persons, living or dead, businesses,
companies, events or locales is entirely coincidental.

This edition published by arrangement with Harlequin Books S.A.

For questions and comments about the quality of this book,
please contact us at CustomerService@Harlequin.com.

Harlequin Enterprises ULC
22 Adelaide St. West, 40th Floor
Toronto, Ontario M5H 4E3, Canada
www.Harlequin.com

Printed in U.S.A.

Julie Anne Lindsey is an obsessive reader who was once torn between the love of her two favorite genres: toe-curling romance and chew-your-nails suspense. Now she gets to write both for Harlequin Intrigue. When she's not creating new worlds, Julie can be found carpooling her three kids around northeastern Ohio and plotting with her shamelessly enabling friends. Winner of the Daphne du Maurier Award for Excellence in Mystery/Suspense, Julie is a member of International Thriller Writers, Romance Writers of America and Sisters in Crime. Learn more about Julie and her books at julieannelindsey.com.

Books by Julie Anne Lindsey

Harlequin Intrigue

Heartland Heroes

SVU Surveillance
Protecting His Witness

Fortress Defense

Deadly Cover-Up
Missing in the Mountains
Marine Protector
Dangerous Knowledge

Garrett Valor

Shadow Point Deputy
Marked by the Marshal

Protectors of Cade County

Federal Agent Under Fire
The Sheriff's Secret

Visit the Author Profile page at Harlequin.com.

CAST OF CHARACTERS

Maisy Daniels—Pregnant witness in protective custody, determined to testify against the man who killed her twin sister.

Blaze Winchester—West Liberty homicide detective, willing to do whatever it takes to protect the woman who's stolen his heart and is carrying his child.

Lucas Winchester—West Liberty special victims detective. Brother to Blaze, Derek and Isaac.

Derek Winchester—Oldest of the Winchester siblings. A PI with an attitude. A rebel and a wild card. Always ready to help his brothers.

Isaac Winchester—Youngest of the four Winchesters. A cousin by blood, brother by upbringing and paramedic by trade. Determined to save the world, one patient at a time.

Sergeant Maxwell—West Liberty police sergeant. Blaze's and Lucas's superior.

Sam Luciano—Organized crime leader. Murderer of Maisy's twin sister, Natalie, among many others.

Chapter One

Maisy Daniels shifted uncomfortably on the hard kitchen chair, rubbing the curve of her once decidedly flat abdomen, which had morphed into a watermelon in her third trimester. She smiled at the thought, not missing her thinner shape at all. Not yet, anyway. Right now her body was doing an amazing feat that many couldn't, and Maisy was honored by the opportunity.

Her baby was stronger by the day, and she couldn't wait to meet the little one soon. She imagined her labor and delivery. The deep, practiced breathing, a positive attitude and classical music playing through each contraction. Her birth plan was perfect, laid out in excruciating detail. Though all that truly mattered was that her baby arrived safely into Maisy's loving embrace, preferably without anyone trying to kill them. In other words, under near-opposite circumstances than those in which her baby was conceived.

"Hey." US Marshal Clara Spencer popped into the small and toasty kitchen with her usual encouraging smile. Her smart blond bob was streaked lightly with gray and tucked behind her ears. Laugh lines hugged the edges of her mouth. "Sorry. I had to take that call. Things are still a go for the move today. We're even moving the timeline up a little. How are you feeling?"

"Good." Maisy straightened in her chair, scrutinizing the woman before her, someone fate had made her dearest friend. One part lawman and two parts Mary Poppins, Clara had become everything to Maisy these last few months, including one of the only people she ever got to see. "The call went okay?" Maisy asked, sensing an odd uncertainty in Clara's normally cheery eyes.

"Mmm-hmm." She patted Maisy's shoulder on her way to the stove, where she'd set a kettle to boil before leaving the room to take a call. "The other marshal will be here within the hour. Then we'll transport you back to your hometown for the trial. You and I will be sharing subpar room service cheeseburgers together in some high-rise hotel by nightfall."

"Wow." Maisy stifled a grimace, forcing

a curt laugh instead. "You make it sound so tempting. I might start walking right now." She curled her arms protectively over her middle, cradling her baby bump. Much as Maisy longed for the trial to be over, her testimony given and Sam Luciano behind bars for life, she would fear for her safety, and that of her baby, until the day officially arrived. Until then, anything could happen, and most of the possibilities running through Maisy's mind were grim.

Sam Luciano was an organized crime boss with reach and influence most celebrities never achieved. She'd come to understand he was involved in every manner of awfulness, but the crime that mattered most to Maisy was the murder of her twin sister, Natalie. And with a little luck, Maisy's testimony would secure Luciano's permanent resident status at the Castle on Cumberland, aka Kentucky State Penitentiary, the state's maximum security and supermax prison.

Clara set a steaming mug of tea on the table before Maisy, its chipped edge and floral pattern worn from age and washing. "Just breathe," she said gently, taking the seat beside her, a second mug cradled in her hands. "You've made it. All the way to the end, and in less than two weeks, you'll be free to go anywhere you want, any time you want and with anyone you choose. No more passing time cooped up in a safe house, playing cards and wearing out the Netflix account with me and your other stuffy old guardians."

"You're not stuffy or old." Maisy smiled, sipping her tea and wondering if it was really that simple. After six long months in near-isolation, she'd tell her story to a jury, justice would prevail and she'd return to her life in progress. It seemed impossible. And suddenly, leaving the place she never wanted to live in the first place felt a lot scarier than she'd ever imagined. "Don't tell the other marshals," Maisy confided, "but I'm going to miss you the most."

Clara set her tea aside. She reached for Maisy and wrapped her in a warm hug. "I'm going to miss you, too, kiddo. But just think, after this is over, our time together will be on your own terms and at your leisure instead of for your protection and under duress."

Maisy nodded, a lump of emotion rising in her throat. The little cottage on Elmwood Lane had been a safe haven for her and the baby she hadn't even known she was carrying on the day she arrived. "I couldn't have survived this without you."

Clara had been everything Maisy needed to

get through life in voluntary captivity, through the shocking realization she would soon be a mother and the oppressive grief of a twin sister lost. She'd been a buoy on days Maisy was sure her testimony wouldn't be enough to make a difference. And she'd found the perfect obstetrician to care for Maisy throughout her pregnancy. She'd driven her to every appointment and nursed Maisy through three long months of morning sickness. She'd done it all without ever being asked.

Maisy wiped a renegade tear as the hug ended, determined to stay strong. "Thank you. For everything."

Clara's brown eyes misted. "Stop that. If you cry, then I'll cry, and the escorting marshal will get here and think we're both nuts."

Maisy did her best to pull herself together, though pregnancy had her emotions thoroughly heightened and her hormones wholly out of whack. "I'll try," she promised, lifting her mug and inhaling the sweet steam before taking a long, soothing sip.

"Good." Clara watched Maisy closely, a small smile budding on her lips. "Did I tell you I was able to poke around a little like you asked?"

"No." A thrill shot through Maisy as she straightened. "Learn anything good?"

"Mostly that I was right, of course. The trial postponements have been in our favor. Prosecution has been building an airtight case. Locating and securing three additional witnesses."

"What?" Maisy set her mug aside so she wouldn't drop it from shock. "There are more witnesses?" A nearly forgotten sense of hope bubbled inside her. She wasn't alone.

"Yes." Clara's grin widened. She'd told her as much before, multiple times, but Maisy had assumed the words were unfounded, meant to make her feel better but with no real basis. "So, it's just like I told you," Clara continued. "Everything is going to be just fine."

"Thank you." Maisy let the tears roll this time, embracing the relief and joy along with a sliver of guilt for asking Clara to nose around outside the scope of the case. "I hope you won't get into trouble for snooping."

"I was careful. And besides, you're being transferred today. The trial is almost here, and this will all be over soon. It was worth the risk just to see that smile on your face." Clara's phone rang, and she glanced at it briefly. Her smile wavered but rallied. "Our ride will be here soon. You should probably finish packing while I take this call."

Maisy rose with her tea and headed to the

small rear bedroom she'd practically lived in since spring, riding on a surge of hope and possibilities. Four witnesses sounded like a pretty strong case to her. Surely no jury would side with Luciano now. And there would be justice for Natalie and all his other victims. Like Aaron.

Maisy sat on the soft twin bed a moment before her trembling legs gave out, and a fresh wave of grief rushed over her. Natalie shouldn't have volunteered to visit Aaron's house that day. He and Maisy had only been on a handful of dates, and he'd nearly thrown Maisy out after taking a private phone call she'd assumed was from a girlfriend. He'd been hiding something, and Maisy had sensed it. She'd left in a huff and forgotten her book. A tattered old copy of *Little Women* she rarely went anywhere without.

Natalie went to retrieve it.

And now she was dead. Her life traded for a ten-dollar paperback.

Maisy's paperback.

She wiped her tears and worked to calm her breathing, fighting to regain control. The unexpected bouts of grief weren't good for her blood pressure, and she needed to think of her baby. "Aunt Natalie was my personal defender," she whispered to her swollen abdomen, imagining her perfect child inside. "Our mama left me that book. She'd read it to us a dozen times and it was her favorite to the end, even through endless rounds of chemo."

Sam Luciano had been at Aaron's house when Natalie arrived. She'd snapped a photo of his car, license plate included, and texted it to Maisy before circling around to the back deck without ringing the doorbell. She'd assumed the car belong to the suspected other woman in Aaron's life, and she'd called to let Maisy know.

"That's how I met your father," Maisy told the bump, now shifting slightly with each stretch of an arm or leg. "He made me feel loved even when I hated myself. He made me smile when all I wanted to do was cry. And he tracked that monster down then arrested him for what he did to Aunt Natalie and Aaron." For the final reason alone, Maisy would love Blaze Winchester until the day she died.

And she'd see him again soon. Seven months pregnant with his child. She'd wanted to tell him sooner but wasn't allowed. Communication with the outside world was limited, and communication with anyone from her past was forbidden, at least until the trial. So Maisy had spent countless nights planning how to break the news. And now she wouldn't have to. A single look at her would say it all.

She pushed onto her feet, forcing Blaze's handsome face from her mind. Whatever he would think of her pregnancy was up to him, and no amount of planning on her part would change it. Until then, she had packing to do.

She'd moved the bulk of her things into a set of plastic bins against the wall when she heard a car outside. A black SUV with tinted glass and a government plate was visible in the driveway, just beyond her first-floor window. The marshal from her home county had arrived to escort her and Clara back to the town where the trial would take place.

A man climbed out from the driver's side, closed his door, then examined the home carefully as he moved toward the porch. He was older, with a dusting of gray at his temples and a scowl in his expression that unsettled Maisy's stomach. Not that it took much for that these days. Blustering November winds tussled his hair and split his unzipped jacket up the center, exposing a sidearm at his hip.

Maisy shivered. Her expression reflected in the windowpane said it all. There was fear and apprehension in her clear hazel eyes and a downward turn to her lips. Even the flush of her pale, freckled skin gave her away. She didn't want to leave. Too many terrible things could happen outside her protected walls, and in her current condition, she was helpless to do more than let them happen if they did.

Cold seemed to seep in from outside, under the locked window and around the reinforced frame. Leeching into Maisy's skin and frosting her bones. According to local news reports, the entirety of northern Kentucky was in for relentless rains this week, followed by dropping temperatures and a heavy late-season snowfall next.

Maisy gave her bare feet, yoga pants and tunic top a regretful look, then headed into the hallway for a coat and her favorite fur-lined boots. The last thing she wanted was to be this pregnant in a snowstorm, but at least she could stay warm while she got through it.

Bang!

The first gunshot sounded before she'd reached the coat hooks in the narrow rear hall.

Clara's voice erupted from the silence a moment later, calling orders and relaying details. Including a description of the man Maisy had seen in the driveway.

Maisy turned, eyes wide and heart pumping as she realized what was happening. Clara was calling for help. The cottage was under attack. "Clara!"

The next gunshot ended Clara's commands.

Fear rooted Maisy in place, freezing her limbs and turning her mind to mush.

The shots began again, this time coming rapidly. Splitting the woodwork of a nearby archway and tossing bits of drywall into the air.

"Clara!" Maisy cried again, this time with all the strength and volume she could muster.

"Run!" Clara answered, weak and frantic. "Run! You know what to do! Go!"

Maisy turned on autopilot. They'd practiced this a dozen times, weekly at first, maybe more. If the cottage was under attack, the marshal on duty would call for backup and hold down the fort. It was Maisy's job to escape. It was her only job in the event of a crisis. *The most important job*, Clara always said. *Because if I die trying to save you, and you're killed anyway, then what was the point?*

Hot tears trailed over Maisy's cheeks, blurring her eyes and stinging her nose as she shoved swollen feet into waiting, unlaced sneakers, swept the go-bag out from beneath the bench at the back door and burst into the frigid windy day, gunshots blazing behind her.

Chapter Two

West Liberty homicide detective Blaze Winchester dragged his weary, aching body away from the precinct where he'd turned a seasoned gangbanger over for booking. The number of kills under the banger's belt was well into double digits, and it felt good to get him off the streets. It had felt less good, however, chasing him eleven blocks through a rival gang's territory, and being sucker punched twice. Blaze's head hurt. His leg muscles burned, and his gut was loudly demanding dinner. Thankfully, his shift was up and there was beer, a marinating rib eye and a warm bed waiting for him at home.

"Hey, Winchester!" Blaze's younger brother's voice rang out behind him. "Wait up."

Lucas waved. The youngest detective with the special victims' unit, he'd been riding the highs of a long-overdue arrest and unexpected reunion with his college sweetheart for months. It was equally good for him and annoying.

Blaze wasn't in the mood.

"Where are you headed?" Lucas asked.

"Home."

"Any news on the Luciano case?" He matched his pace with Blaze as they moved through the lot toward their waiting trucks.

The air seemed to thicken at the sound of Sam Luciano's name, the world going colder and darker. "No." Blaze hadn't heard anything new and nothing official. Everyone who did know anything was infuriatingly tight-lipped on the matter. But the last time he'd checked in with the guards where Luciano awaited trial, they were distinctly on edge. One guard admitted there was new tension among the inmates but couldn't say why. He described a vague but hostile undercurrent he couldn't quite put his finger on, but he was sure the other guards felt it, too. *Something*, he'd said, *like the brewing of a storm*. The guard felt certain that Luciano was the eye of that storm but had no idea what he was up to. Blaze had a guess, and he didn't like it. Luciano knew the prosecution had him dead to rights this time, and he was surely plotting a way to save his sorry behind. There hadn't been any news after that, if he could call it news at all. And the trial was less than two weeks away.

"You want to hit O'Grady's Pub?" Lucas asked. "I heard you had one hell of a day, and it looks like you're getting a shiner. Beer could help."

Blaze grimaced, his cheekbone aching on cue. "No, thanks."

O'Grady's was a place Lucas spent a lot of time in college and still did on occasion. He and his fiancée liked to hang out there—it reminded them of the old days. Neither brother enjoyed the local cop bars, so they met there a couple nights a week. This week, Blaze had too much on his mind to socialize. When he wasn't working, he was preparing mentally for Luciano's trial, where he would take the stand. "I'm grilling and watching the game tonight. You're welcome to tag along if you want to split a rib eye."

Lucas laughed. "Like you'd ever split a rib eye. Anyway, I've got dinner plans. I just wanted to make sure you're okay."

Blaze waved him off. "I'm fine. Tired. Hungry. Fine." He repeated the initial sentiment slowly for emphasis. Then, before Lucas could push, Blaze let the grouchy expression of an older brother being coddled by his younger sibling creep over his face.

Lucas lifted his palms and stepped back, easing in the direction of his vehicle parked several spots away. "You know Gwen has friends if you're ever interested in going out and acting your age again sometime. Nice friends. Redheads, even." He grinned suggestively.

"Good night." Blaze climbed inside his truck and shut the door. The only redhead Blaze wanted to spend time with was locked away in witness protection and probably hadn't given him a second thought since she'd arrived. He turned over the engine and powered down his window, hooking an elbow over the frame. "Tell Gwen I said hello and that I'm sorry I can't go to O'Grady's. Now she's stuck with you all night. I owe her one."

"Funny," Lucas said, climbing into the seat of his own truck and not looking as if he thought it was funny at all. "You know being alone will make you bitter," he hollered.

"Too late." Blaze closed the window and pumped the heat.

Temperatures had been falling all day, and if the sway of the trees and tint of the sky were any indication, the thin drizzle starting now would soon become a storm.

Blaze followed Lucas as far as the highway before honking his goodbye. Lucas took the on-ramp toward the restored historical home he shared with Gwen. Blaze stayed the course, riding the two-lane road out of town, headed for his cabin outside city limits.

He adjusted his wipers as the rain picked up, his mind wandering back to Luciano's trial the way it always did these days. Blaze had made the arrest no one before him had ever been able to achieve, and his career could be made if the trial went his way. If not, he'd have reason to worry. Luciano was smoke, and he controlled the better part of Kentucky's underground—probably a few cops and officials, too. So, if he got out, or even stayed in his current digs, where he might regain some control on the outside, there would be hell to pay for dragging him through this. And Blaze had more than just himself to worry about.

The trial had already been pushed back twice. Not a good sign, and possibly Luciano's doings. There were rumors of threats made against the prosecution and the judge, but no one would say, officially. No one who knew anything about Luciano wanted to be anywhere near that trial. Fear his crime family would retaliate on participants was strong, but it wouldn't stop Blaze from taking the stand. Nothing would. As far as he was concerned, there wasn't a hole deep enough for Luciano, and he'd do anything to help throw him in it.

Blaze hit the defrosters and cranked the heat inside his truck as homes grew smaller and the streetlights more sparse. Slowly, the two-lane road through town became a winding country route with sporadic traffic and an endless tree line.

By the time he hit the long gravel drive to his cabin, Blaze was well past the need for a beer or a steak. Thoughts of Luciano had wound him tight enough to implode, and with no one around to punch or chase, a good night's sleep was probably what he needed most. He could eat tomorrow when his mood improved. For now he was glad to put the day behind him and mentally mark another off his internal count-down to Luciano's trial.

He left his truck in the drive and turned for his steps, pulling the hood of his jacket higher over his head against the pelting rain. Something moved on his porch, and Blaze's body went rigid, his hand straight to his sidearm. If someone planned to keep him from testifying, they'd quickly regret it. "Who's there?" he demanded, widening his stance and ready to draw.

"Blaze?" a small, familiar voice quavered

in the shadows. "It's me. I'm sorry. I should have called."

Blaze blinked against the darkness, his heart pinching tight. "Maisy?"

Maisy Daniels had torn into his life late last year like a bullet, ripping past all his walls and pretenses. She'd helped him track down and arrest Luciano for the murder of a friend and her twin sister, then vanished with a band of US Marshals. Taken in for protection until the trial. Luciano had been the catalyst who'd brought Maisy into his life, then the reason she was taken away. And he hated him all the more for the latter.

Blaze flew onto the porch, drawn by shock and the heartbreak in her voice. She was huddled in the corner, arms curled around herself and thick red hair hanging wet and dark against her cheeks. "What happened? What are you doing here?" He scanned the empty space near his truck for signs of another vehicle he'd somehow missed. Sudden fear clenched his heart and lungs. "Where are the marshals?"

"Dead, I think," Maisy whispered, rolling pleading, tear-filled eyes to meet his. "I didn't know where else to go."

He reached for her, gut wrenching. "Let's get you inside. You're soaked, probably frozen and…" His words were lost as she stretched onto her feet and her distended silhouette registered in his addled mind. "Pregnant?"

MAISY FOUGHT AGAINST the urge to throw herself at Blaze, to thank him in tears and hugs and sobs for not turning her away. She knew, logically, of course, that as the arresting detective for Sam Luciano, Blaze would never turn away a witness who could help the case. But Blaze was so much more than some detective to her, and the intimate physical connection they'd once shared made everything deeply, illogically personal, even now. She forced her chin up as he led her inside.

The small, familiar cabin hadn't changed. She'd loved the open floor plan the first time she'd visited, but after months in a highly compartmentalized safe house, the cabin's layout seemed dangerous. There was nowhere to hide. Only a single bedroom and bathroom at the back of the home had doors to block an intruder's view. The living room, dining room and kitchen were all visible from the welcome mat where she stood.

She took a tentative step forward, marveling at how well the scene before her matched her memories. The ashy evidence of an appreciated fireplace. Piles of paperwork on the desk in the corner. Blaze's cologne woven into the fabric of his furniture, curtains and rugs. It was as if his home had been frozen in time. As if she'd never left.

If only that was true.

Blaze locked the door behind her, checked the window, then ran a heavy hand through sopping brown hair. The wind had knocked his hood off as he'd run to her, and he hadn't seemed to notice. His long legs had eaten up the space between them. His expression had been fearful, but exuberant. Until she'd stood. And everything had changed. "Let's take care of you first," he said. "Then we'll talk about what's happening. Obviously you weren't followed. If you had been, you wouldn't still be here." He grimaced, then stripped out of his coat, dropping it onto the arm of his couch as he darted through his living room then vanished into the bathroom. "Are you hurt? Sick?" he called, riffling through the linen cabinet.

"No."

He reappeared a moment later with a stack of towels. "Hang on."

He opened the door to his bedroom and hurried inside. Dresser drawers squeaked and thumped in the distance while she shivered on the black-and-white-checkered rug inside his door, trying not to make a puddle on the wide-planked wooden floor. "Okay." Blaze reappeared with a pile of clothing stacked on the towels and extended the offering as he crossed the living area to her. "You probably want a hot shower, but I think we should talk first. I can wait if you want to change. I don't want you to be uncomfortable." His gaze moved pointedly to her middle before jumping back to her eyes.

Too late to avoid being uncomfortable, she thought, cradling her belly in her arms. "Thanks."

"Maybe you should sit."

"First I'll change," she said, accepting the towels and clothing. "I'll only be a minute."

He swept one arm in the general direction she was headed. "Take your time. I'll put on the coffee. Oh. Maisy?"

She paused midstep, her heart beating wildly. Was this the moment he would ask about her baby? About *their* baby?

"Is caffeine okay?" He looked to her middle again. "I mean, you know, for…you?"

Maisy sighed, relieved to put off the inevitable a few moments longer. "Whatever you make is perfect. Thank you."

He nodded, and she hurried away.

Inside the bathroom, Maisy stripped out of her things, soaked to the bone from a long walk in the wind and rain. She hung her shirt and pants over the shower curtain rod to dry.

There had been a time, however briefly, when she'd showered in this room as often as her own. Her toothbrush had stood with his on the counter, and she'd even kept a few things in a drawer.

Maisy traced a finger along that drawer, then tugged nosily, wondering if maybe… But no. Apparently some things at Blaze's home had changed after all. The drawer was empty. Nothing inside but her memories, and she wondered for the millionth time if Blaze had thought of her at all while she was gone.

She dried herself with the towels, mopping rain from her hair before sliding into the clothes he'd provided. Elastic-waisted sweatpants, a large T-shirt and hoodie. She tugged white athletic socks over her frozen feet, then gave her flushed face a long, appraising look in the bathroom mirror. The day had been awful, and it showed. Every part of her ached, from her heart to her toes, and now, on this worst day of all, she had to explain her pregnancy to Blaze. She'd hoped that the news would make him happy, but how could this moment ever feel good or right in the shadows of such loss and desperation?

A soft rap on the door startled her back to the moment. "You okay in there?"

She wiped hot tears from her cheeks, then

pulled in a steadying breath before opening the door. "Sorry. It's been a tough day."

He nodded, giving her a once-over, then offering a steaming cup. "I decided against coffee."

She batted back another round of tears as she inhaled the familiar scent of chamomile tea. The same tea Clara had made her only hours before. "Thank you."

"I called around while you were changing, but no one's talking about what happened to you today." He stepped aside to let her out of the bathroom. "Luciano's determined to stop this trial. He's been making threats from behind bars, and I'm willing to bet he's moved on to taking action." He turned worried gray-blue eyes on her as they moved toward the kitchen together. "Did you tell anyone about us? About our relationship before?"

"Just Clara," she said, feeling his words like a punch to the gut. Was he embarrassed? Ashamed? "She was the marshal who was with me today." A wedge of grief lodged in her throat, and she had to work to force it away.

He shook his head. "I'm sorry."

Maisy sipped her tea, longing for the warmth of it to erase her bone-deep chill. "We shouldn't tell anyone if no one is talking," she said. "We can't trust the marshals. It was a marshal who attacked today. There's no way to know who can be trusted. If you ask too many questions, someone will figure out I'm with you."

"If they haven't already," he said. "You're sure you never told anyone about us?"

"Only Clara," Maisy repeated, more firmly this time. "Lucas knew about us," she said, biting into her lip and begging the pain in her heart to relocate. She stopped when she tasted blood, then winced.

"Yes, and he's digging into this for me. Quietly. Until he calls back, let's go over everything you can remember. Walk me through your day. Are you hungry?"

"No." Maisy's stomach growled in protest of the lie.

"How do you feel about steak?"

She shrugged, unsure she could manage anything so heavy and hoping the tea would stay down. "Do you have toast?"

"Sure. I'll cook. You talk," he said, pushing up the sleeves on a navy thermal shirt and washing his hands.

Maisy took a seat at Blaze's small kitchen table, then steeled herself to relive the events of her day. She covered it all, from the sweet moments shared with Clara to the marshal's morning phone calls. Two in the time it had taken to have a cup of tea. The arrival of the second marshal. The shooting. And the running.

Maisy had escaped with her go-bag, bare feet stuffed into sneakers, a tunic top and yoga pants only, through icy winds and falling temperatures to the bus stop at Fourth and Walnut. Clara had forced her to memorize the schedules of buses nearest the safe house. "It was already after one when I left," she said, "so I'd missed the bus on Frank by ten minutes. I had to double back and cross the block to Fourth. I used the alley entrance to a dry cleaner's as cover until I saw the bus approaching."

The gunshots had echoed in her ears as she'd run. Police cruisers and emergency vehicles had raced past, responding to Clara's calls. Hoping to save her and arrest the male marshal whose face Maisy would never forget. "I took the local bus to a stop near the Greyhound station, then bought a ticket to Cincinnati," she continued. "Clara said that if I did that, anyone who was following me would assume I was planning to hide, trying to disappear across state lines. I took taxis from there. A few miles at a time, walking as far as I could in between rides so that even the cabbies wouldn't know where I went once they dropped me off. When I made it back to West Liberty, I got out at the church on Mogadore Road and walked the rest of the way."

Blaze pressed the lever on his toaster, lowering two slices of bread into the heat. "You walked from St. Peter's? I live nearly four miles from there."

"And it took me the rest of the day," she said. Her blistered feet could attest. "I stopped as often as possible to get off my feet and have something to drink."

"Drink?" he said. "Not eat?"

She shook her head. "There was only a little cash left once I'd paid for the buses and cabbies."

Blaze opened the refrigerator and took out a carton of eggs, a bag of shredded cheese and pile of vegetables. "You still like omelets?"

"Yes." Heat rushed to her cheeks as she answered. Several mornings when she'd worn his T-shirt and little else flashed to mind. Just Blaze in pajama bottoms, pushing eggs around a skillet while she did her best to tease and distract him.

She'd held on to those memories tightly during her time at the safe house. The time she'd spent with Blaze had been intense, hot and all-encompassing. A necessary release and distraction when emotions had ruled her life. Grief, shame and guilt over the loss of her sister, who'd been doing a simple favor. Anger, anguish and fear related to Luciano, what he'd done to Natalie and Aaron and what he would do to Maisy if given the chance. She'd knotted all those things up tight and shoved them down deep in order to stay strong and help Blaze locate the psychopath. But they'd leaked out in the forms of need and desire. Her lust for Blaze had created an outlet so emotionally satisfying and physically exhausting that she'd held herself together between the rounds just to get her next hit. Then, before she'd realized, months had passed, Luciano was under arrest and she was on her way to an undisclosed location, where she would await her time to testify. Now, here she was, faced with all the emotions again, and without an outlet. Feeling alone in a room with the man who'd once been her refuge.

Blaze worked efficiently at his counter, making her meal exactly as he used to and checking his phone regularly between chops and stirs. He delivered the toast when it popped up, with a mini tub of butter and a knife, then turned on the evening news.

"Thank you." She bit into the first slice of warm toast before bothering to add butter. Her mouth watered and her stomach groaned in appreciation. She rested a hand over her bump as she felt her baby begin to stir. "This is delicious."

Blaze cocked a brow as the eggs cooked. "It's toast."

The phone rang and he stilled. "It's Lucas." He accepted the call, then flipped the omelet that was slowly filling the small home with heavenly aromas of salty cheese and all the best veggies. Onions. Sweet peppers. Mushrooms.

Maisy finished the first slice of toast and moved quickly to the second.

Blaze spoke in acronyms and painfully short sentences for several seconds before disconnecting the call. He plated the eggs, then made his way to the table, setting one plate before her, keeping the second for himself. "The marshals made the official announcement," he said. "Two units assigned to the protection of a Luciano witness failed to check in. They've alerted local police to the situation and given a physical description of a male marshal, still missing."

"And Clara?" she asked, her stomach turning.

He shook his head. "Eat. You need the fuel." His gaze traveled to her hand, resting on her rounded middle. "And the nutrition."

She squirmed under his scrutiny, trying desperately not to think of Clara, hoping there was a chance she wasn't really gone.

Blaze narrowed his eyes, squinted at Maisy's

bump, and she could see him doing the mental math. Working out if the baby could be his, or if she'd somehow gotten involved with another man after leaving town. Maisy nearly laughed.

Blaze lifted his fork. "Lucas is calling back when he knows something more."

"You told him I was here?" she asked, knowing the truth. There were few secrets between the Winchester brothers.

"Yeah." Again his attention lowered to the hand resting on her abdomen.

"And you told him I'm pregnant?"

He gave one short, stiff dip of his chin in answer, then dragged his gaze to meet hers. "You want to tell me about that?" he asked, his expression guarded and mildly hostile. Or maybe that was her projecting.

"I learned I was pregnant about two weeks after I arrived at the safe house."

His furrowed brows relaxed slowly. "Two weeks."

"Yes." She took her time forking a bite of omelet before meeting his eye once more. "At first I didn't realize what was happening. All the grief and guilt and emotion I'd been avoiding hit hard once I had nothing to do but think. Then I got a stomach bug." Her lips twitched as the evening round of in utero kickboxing began.

"Morning sickness," he guessed.

"Yes."

He lowered his fork to his plate. "Is the baby mine?" he asked carefully, voice wary.

"Yes."

Blaze covered his mouth with one big hand, scrubbing it across his lips and cheek before dropping it into his lap. "A boy? Girl?"

Maisy shook her head. "I don't know." She'd forgone the information in favor of waiting for Blaze. He'd already missed so much by the time the baby was old enough to determine the gender, she'd wanted to save something for him to experience with her instead of after the fact. She'd wanted to include him, if he wanted to be included, because she knew it would break her heart if the tables were turned and she was the one finding out at the last minute that she would be a mother and that she'd missed everything leading up to that moment.

"What are you waiting for?" he asked.

"You." The word was barely more than a whisper on her tongue. Her eyes stung with the truth and vulnerability in that single word.

Their gazes locked for one brief moment, the way they had so many times before.

"Why didn't you tell me?" he asked, looking crestfallen. And sounding a little angry.

Maisy recoiled. "How could I?" She searched his expression for a hint on how to proceed. Was he truly upset? With the news? With her? The prospect unnerved her further, and her spine straightened. "I wasn't allowed to use a phone. I couldn't leave the house for days. I've spent the last six months in a one-thousand-square-foot home, under constant guard of strangers. I looked forward to the doctor appointments just so I could get out, see and talk to people who weren't bound by their job and an oath to protect me. It's not as if I've been living it up. Laughing about the big secret I was keeping. I was isolated, Blaze, and you know it. You're the one who sent me there."

His jaw clenched. "I made the arrangements to keep you safe."

"Yeah?" she laughed humorlessly, pushing away from the table. "How did that work out?"

Maisy walked away as calmly as she could manage while fighting a scream and possibly more tears. Back to the bathroom where she could close the door and press her hands against her ears, where Clara's voice still rang. *If I die trying to save you, and you're killed anyway, then what was the point?*

It was a good question, because Maisy couldn't see the point in any of this.

Chapter Three

Blaze watched Maisy walk away, his heart pounding and thoughts racing. Aside from the shocking realization that she was in serious danger again, maybe even more danger than when she left town to start with, now she was pregnant. With his baby.

His head spun as the bathroom door snapped shut behind her, and he let his head fall forward into waiting palms. A torrent of frustration and curses poured from his lips. No surprise she'd taken his anger personally. He could barely put two coherent thoughts together, let alone a decent encouraging sentence. Was that what she needed? Encouragement?

He raised his head with a groan. How could he possibly know what Maisy needed beyond protection? They'd been apart longer than they'd ever been together. And the fact that she'd gone through this much of her pregnancy alone, displaced, afraid, and now with a lunatic gunning for her all over again. *Not just her*, he thought, *them. Maisy and our baby.* His hands curled into fists at the final thought. And the curses started once more.

Why hadn't the marshals in charge of her contacted him about the baby? How had they watched her, with his child growing inside her, and not found a way to pass the message along? He was a detective, for crying out loud. He understood the stakes and the system. He wouldn't have done anything to give away her position or put her in harm's way. He'd do anything to protect her. *Them*, he corrected himself with the shake of his head. Sure, he would've wanted to pass a message back to her. Tell her he was happy and that she shouldn't be afraid. He might've tried to arrange a call to be sure she knew he meant it, or a visit…

Maybe they were right to keep him in the dark. Because how could he have sat idly by when he wanted to write in stone that he was all in for his kid? No matter what happened between him and Maisy.

The sound of running water drew his attention back to the bathroom, where it seemed Maisy had taken him up on the offer of a hot shower. Good. She needed time to warm up and unwind. He needed time to cool down and make a plan.

Soapy scents of his cheap, drugstore shampoo crept under the door as he began to pace. It was easier to think when he was in motion. Maisy would hate the subpar, nearly empty selection of bath products jammed into the caddy. He'd packed up her things months ago, hating the way remnants of the fruity, floral soaps and lotions seemed to linger. For weeks, she'd been everywhere he looked, and he couldn't stand it when she wasn't. So, he'd packed her up, memories, toiletries and all. And put it all in a box, out of sight and out of mind, where he wasn't tempted to dwell on things he couldn't change.

It had been stupid and unprofessional of him to get involved with a witness. He knew it then, and he knew it now, but there had always been something about that woman. Something that had tangled his thoughts, then his body, with hers so easily and intensely. Something he could never put a name to. Then she was gone. He'd never felt that way before or since. And darn if that same whatever it was wasn't back full force at the sight of her. It wasn't right, or fair, that all his wishes to see her one more time had been granted by a cruel twist of fate. Wasn't fair that Maisy was back, but she was in danger.

And probably naked in his shower.

The idea of her new, fuller silhouette looming behind his shower curtain flashed into his imagination, and his jaw dropped.

He dialed Lucas.

"Hey," his brother answered before the first ring had finished, as if he'd already had the phone in his hands. "I was just about to call you. The word is officially out on Maisy. Marshals contacted the precinct. You'll be getting a call any minute. Sergeant Maxwell's freaking out. Luciano's conviction was supposed to be a gold star on his career right along with yours."

Blaze paused to consider that. "It's not over yet. We'll still get Luciano. What do you think happened to get the marshals talking?" Surely they hadn't simply changed their minds on sharing the fact one of their own attacked a safe house today.

"I don't know, but Blaze," Lucas began, hesitant. "Is the baby yours?"

His mind snapped back to the moment, torn between all-encompassing fear and elation. "Yeah." He cleared his throat against the strange thickness and marveled briefly at the way his chest filled with pride.

"Congratulations, big brother," Lucas said. "How's that going so far?"

Blaze flicked his attention to the closed bathroom door. "Not great."

His phone buzzed with an incoming call,

and he checked the number on the screen. "That's Maxwell. I've got to go." He disconnected with Lucas, shifting easily between the calls and noting the shower had stopped in the background. "Winchester."

"I've got some tough news on the Luciano case," Sergeant Maxwell began, skipping the customary greeting and unnecessary introduction. "The witness you moved into protection this spring is missing, along with the US marshal assigned to assist in her transportation. Another marshal, who we believe was protecting her at the time of the disappearance, was fatally wounded."

Blaze returned to pacing. "You're sure the protective marshal is dead?" he asked, deciding how much of what he knew to tell his sergeant.

"Yes," Maxwell answered. "Marshal Clara Spencer suffered multiple gunshot wounds to the chest and torso. She was already gone when backup arrived. We're hoping the other marshal was able to get Miss Daniels to safety, but considering it's been hours since he last checked in, no one is holding out a lot of hope."

Blaze slowed his orbit around the kitchen table. "You think the transporting marshal saved the witness from the shooter?"

"It's the best-case scenario," Maxwell said,

his voice low and unsure. "So, that's what we're hoping. I'll keep you posted."

"Great." Blaze pressed the palm of one hand to his forehead. "I'd appreciate that."

"I know your shift just ended, but I want you doing whatever you can to stay on top of this. We can't let this case fall apart. So let's be proactive. Find out where Miss Daniels might go or who she might talk to if she's separated from the marshal. The trial's coming up fast, and we're down two witnesses. You need to get Daniels back into protective custody."

Blaze ground his teeth. "Protective custody didn't work so well earlier today. How do we know she'll be safe if we go that route again?"

The bathroom door opened, and Maisy stepped out. The mirror was steamed behind her. She'd redressed in his clothes, filling out the tops in the center now, sleeves hanging low over her small hands and baggy sweatpants bunched up at the ankles of her short legs. Her skin was flushed from the warmth of the water. Her hair damp and wild.

"I don't know, Winchester," he bellowed. "But I've got protocols to follow, and so do you. So start working every angle."

Blaze lifted a finger to his lips when he caught Maisy's eye, suddenly certain of how much he wanted to share with Maxwell.

Nothing. Not yet.

"Sergeant?" Something the older man had said returned to Blaze with a snap, and he felt his brows pulling low. "Did you say we're down to two witnesses?" He hoped he'd misunderstood. The prosecution's case relied on the presence and credibility of their witnesses. "There were four." Losing two would be devastating.

Blaze watched as the beautiful redhead drifted closer to him, fearful for new reasons now. Losing more than one witness meant something bigger than he'd imagined was afoot, and that was no good for Maisy.

She stopped moving. Tension stiffened her posture, and fear flashed in her eyes.

"That's the other update we were given," Maxwell said. "William Hanes was found dead in his SUV this morning. Outside his office in Louisville. Hanes was an informant from Luciano's batch of thugs. No one was supposed to know he was turning on him at trial."

Blaze felt his muscles lock. This was more than Luciano becoming privy to Maisy's location and taking a chance to silence her. This was a multitiered attack. "Luciano's eliminating the witnesses."

Maisy lowered herself onto Blaze's worn-out sofa and pulled the quilt off the back, a gift, she remembered, from his mother. "Luciano's killing witnesses," she said, raising her eyes to Blaze as he moved into the living room, having ended his call.

He took a seat at her side. "It appears that way."

Her arms went around her middle on instinct, and she told herself to breathe.

"According to my sergeant, the local marshals think the man who came to transport you might've taken you away with him for your protection."

"What?" Maisy's jaw sank open. "If that guy saved me, then who do they think was the shooter?"

Blaze lifted his shoulder slightly, lips pursed. "Didn't say."

Anger rushed in Maisy's veins. "That guy's not a hero. He's a killer."

Blaze's knee began to bob, and he kneaded his hands on his lap. His gray-blue eyes were soft and compassionate when he turned to her. "I asked about your friend Clara."

"She didn't make it," Maisy guessed, reading the grim expression on his brow.

"I'm sorry. No."

The introductory notes of a special report interrupted the evening news, and Maisy and Blaze turned to it in unison. "This just in," an anchor proclaimed from his position on the courthouse steps. Behind him, an enormous American flag waved in the wind and rain.

Maisy's pulse thumped between her ears as the reporter recounted details of the Luciano case. And she cringed as he relayed facts from her nightmarish day. Tears welled as Clara's death was announced, matter-of-factly, and backdropped by a photo of her with her family.

"Maisy," Blaze said softly, the sound of her name on his lips spilling goose pimples over her flesh. "Are you okay?"

She nodded quickly, fighting tears. The concern in his voice nearly broke her, but she'd already lost too many hours to grief today.

Now it was time to be strong. She'd assumed earlier that if the safe house ever came under siege, she'd be helpless. But she'd proven herself wrong. She'd run. Executed the plan the marshals had put in place. Though, she'd improvised at the end, seeking Blaze's protection instead of calling the local marshals' office as she'd been taught. After a marshal had killed Clara, Blaze was the only person she knew she could trust. Still, Maisy had saved herself and her baby. She would keep being strong and help Blaze make sure Luciano was punished for the lives he'd taken. The crime boss probably thought he was saving himself with this sudden strike of aggression, but in reality, he was digging his own grave. Or supermax jail cell, as it may be.

"You don't have to testify, you know," Blaze said. "No one would blame you if you decided not to. You have a baby to think about now, someone else to put first. And seeing Luciano punished isn't worth risking your life. Or the life of your baby."

Maisy smoothed the soft material of his hoodie over the curve of her middle, inhaling the scent of him and trying not to scream. "I'm absolutely testifying," she said, forcing her shoulders back and her frustrations down. "I owe it to Natalie. To Aaron. To Clara. And to all the other people whose lives were taken because of Luciano." And she owed it to all the people who'd eventually become his victim if he wasn't locked away for good. "You said the prosecution is down a witness. That leaves me and two others, and it means my testimony is more important than ever now."

His jaw clenched. "And what about the baby?"

"What about the baby?" She bristled. "I'm doing this for the baby. Because what kind of mother would I be if I didn't do the right thing now, when it matters the most? And lives are on the line?"

"You'd be the kind of mother who's alive to raise her baby," he said. "One who has a child to raise because she kept them both out of harm's way."

Her blood boiled at the suggestion. And at the words *her baby*. Hers. Not his. "Don't you dare do that," she snapped. "Don't make me out to be selfish or careless. I'm not either of those things. And what about you, Detective Winchester? Are you out of harm's way? Or is your life on the line every day that you get up and put on that badge?" She crossed her arms and narrowed her eyes. "What kind of father does that make you?"

"I'm not pregnant," he snapped.

"And I'm not helpless. The least I can do is show up at court, like I promised, and tell Natalie's story. In fact, that's the one and only thing I can do to get justice for my sister. And I'm sure as heck going to do it. With or without your help."

His expression soured, then ran the gamut of emotions, from suppressed outrage to something resembling compassion, before going flat. Settling on the blank cop expression she hated.

"A marshal came into my safe house and killed my friend," she went on, sternly, determined to make him see things her way. "Luciano knows who I am and that I planned to testify. He won't stop coming for me if I promise not to. I made his list, which means I'm in danger until his hands are permanently tied. I don't know who I can trust, and I don't know who will help me if you won't, but I'll still try because I have to."

The forgotten newscast returned from a commercial, and the anchor, still poised on the courthouse steps, said her name. A photo of Maisy lodged in the bottom right corner of the screen.

Blaze cursed. He fished the remote from a basket on the table and pumped up the volume. "Looks like news travels fast."

"West Liberty local Maisy Daniels," the reporter continued, "set to testify in the Sam Luciano trial late next week, has allegedly gone missing from her safe house. Daniels was scheduled to return to town today for preparation with the prosecution, but neither she nor the US marshal assigned to her have reported to their destination."

A second photo appeared on screen, taking up residence in the opposite corner. "Gene Franco, a longtime member of the US Marshals service and local resident, was sent to collect Miss Daniels," the reporter explained. The smiling man in the photo wore an official uniform jacket and hat. Happy eyes stared joy-ously into the camera, a striking jolt of blue against the backdrop of ivory skin and a mass of white hair. Clean shaven with a full, round face, this man could've been anyone's dad or grandpa, maybe a neighbor or friend, but he definitely wasn't the one who'd come to her safe house. "That's not him," Maisy whispered, confusion circling in her chest.

"What?" Blaze's bouncy knee stilled. "What do you mean?"

"I mean that's not the man who came for me." She swung a pointed finger toward the screen. "It wasn't him."

Blaze stretched onto his feet, rubbing a hand over his mouth, then locking the open palm onto his hip. "So this guy isn't corrupt."

"I don't know about that, but he's definitely not the man who shot Clara." Maisy stared back at the jolly-looking man in the photo, suddenly saddened by what his disappear-ance likely meant for him. "And he's prob-ably dead."

Blaze laced his fingers on top of his head. "If we don't have a murderous marshal on our hands, we're probably dealing with a hired gun."

"A hit man?" Maisy squeaked. Were those

even real? Criminals, yes. Corrupt lawmen, sure. But hit men?

"Maybe," he said. "Luciano's facing life in the supermax, and it looks like he's pulling out all the stops to make sure that doesn't happen."

Chapter Four

Maisy woke to the scents of eggs and bacon. She curled and stretched beneath the thick down comforter, content and utterly at peace. For one blissful moment, before opening her eyes, she was back at the safe house, counting the last few days before she would return to West Liberty and give testimony that would finally put Sam Luciano in prison. Her dreams of pending freedom and safety, for her and for her baby, grew with each new breath. She could almost hear her dear friend Clara humming in the kitchen.

Clara.

Maisy's heart kicked and reality snapped her eyes wide. The familiar ache of grief wedged in her throat and weighted her chest. She wasn't at the safe house, and Clara would never again make breakfast. Not for Maisy, and not for the family she'd left behind. A too-big sacrifice made in the name of protecting Maisy and her baby.

Tears blurred her vision as the wave of emotion crashed over her. Another woman was dead because of Maisy. First Natalie. Now Clara. And the gaping holes left by their absences were too much to bear.

She pressed her face into the pillow, willing back the breakdown that had been looming since she'd opened the safe house door and run. Since she'd left Clara behind. Maisy owed Clara's family everything for their loss, but how could she even begin to repay that debt? She released the pillow on a long, shuddering breath. Maisy would have to carry this grief with her, like the rest, because there would be no amends for the devastation she'd caused. She'd just have to make sure her shoulders were strong enough to carry the burden.

Her heart ached as she swung her feet over the bed's edge and onto the floor. She couldn't rewind time, and she could never thank Clara's family properly or enough. But she could make sure her sacrifice meant something. She could follow through with her testimony and see Luciano punished.

She could stop him from taking more lives.

Her stomach grumbled in response to the savory-scented breakfast down the hall, and she forced herself upright. Then shuffled into Blaze's bathroom to prepare for the day, whatever it would bring. She'd slept deeply for the first time in months, thanks to the emotional stress of a narrow escape and the physical exertion of many miles walked. The haystack masquerading as her hair and sheet marks pressed into her cheeks confirmed it. She looked longingly at the shower, dreaming of the hot water against her skin, but her baby had other plans, twisting and kicking in a rhythm that could only be interpreted as a plea for bacon.

She brushed her teeth and hair, warmed by the fact Blaze had kept her old things after all, then followed the scents of breakfast to the kitchen. Her steps faltered when her abdomen tightened and the ache of a false contraction rippled over her. She leaned against the wall and rubbed her bump, breathing slowly through the dull pain. Braxton-Hicks contractions were the newest in a long line of bizarre things her body had done these last few months, each meant to accommodate and one day deliver her baby. "I know you're excited to get out here and meet me," she whispered, catching her breath and soothing her infant, "but I need you to wait until this trial is over." It was a conversation she'd been having more and more. "You're going to be just fine where you are until then, okay? Don't rush."

Eager as she was to finally see and kiss her baby's perfect cherub face, she really didn't want to give her testimony from a delivery room. Though she suspected a hospital gown might be the only thing that would fit her if she got any bigger.

Still, a hospital wasn't safe. Nowhere was. Not if Luciano had gotten to her at a federal safe house. Going into labor before the trial would mean becoming a sitting duck. An immobile target. Easy pickings. And if she survived long enough to safely deliver her baby, then be released, she'd be on the run with a newborn, and that was her personal nightmare.

She peeled herself off the wall and went to greet Blaze.

"Morning," she said, taking a moment to savor the perfection of him at the stove, a fitted heather-gray T-shirt and low-slung jeans clinging in all the right places. His hair was damp and mussed from a shower. His feet were bare. And that smile when he saw her sent her heart into an erratic sprint.

"Hey." He flipped off the stove's burners, then let his gaze slide over her. "Hungry?"

She nodded, hoping he couldn't read her

mind. The food smelled amazing, but her body was suddenly craving more than breakfast.

"Have a seat. It's ready," he said, plating the meal onto matching dishes, then delivering them to the table. "Tea or water?"

"Tea?" she asked, scanning the stove for signs of a kettle.

Blaze delivered a pot and mug with tea bag. "Hot and ready when you are."

Heat rushed across her cheeks, and she couldn't stop a little grin from curling her lips. "Ready. Thanks." Her tummy fluttered with the pleasure of his attention. She poured a cup, trying uselessly to concentrate on anything besides the memories of just how attentive Blaze could be.

"Sleep well?" he asked, joining her at the table.

Her mind raced with faded images of him. Memories from another life, when he'd lavished her with his undivided attention and unhurried time. Their bodies tangled and sliding together beneath his sheets.

"What are you thinking about?" he asked.

Maisy paused her chewing, cheeks flashing hot once more. She took her time before answering. First sipping, then swallowing her tea. "Everything's delicious," she said. "I dropped into your lap yesterday, on the run from a psychopath and carrying your child. And you're handling it all with complete Zen."

"Maybe I have you fooled," he said, flashing a brief, but brilliant smile. "Maybe breakfast is just a ploy for your time and information."

She shook her head slowly. "You always made me breakfast."

His head tipped slightly over one shoulder, and his gaze darted to her mouth. "I've always wanted your time."

Maisy didn't bother to hide her smile. "Okay. So, what can I do for you?"

He pulled his eyes back to meet hers. "When are you due?"

"Ah." She sipped her tea, pleased he was interested in the baby. Terrified he wasn't happy about it. He hadn't really said one way or another. "Six weeks. Give or take."

His eyes widened momentarily, then dropped to her middle before returning to meet hers. "That's soon. When did you find out and how?"

"A couple weeks after I got to the safe house. I'd been sick. I mentioned that last night."

He nodded. "I remember. Tell me more."

She squared her shoulders and settled her hands on the bump. "I assumed all my symptoms were stress related. It was a tough time for me. Fatigue, lack of appetite, heightened emotions." She shook her head. "Even when I realized I was late for my cycle, I dismissed it as stress related. It was another week or two before I was willing to face the fact I could be pregnant. We'd been so careful." She shivered at a flash of them together, joined by hearts and bodies. She'd been falling in love. Fast, deep and powerless to stop it. "I had to ask one of the marshals to buy a home test kit for me. That was humiliating, because they all knew my previous few months were spent trying to find Luciano, and always with you, the detective assigned to my twin's murder case." The words soured on her tongue, turning her stomach, hating the reminder Natalie was gone. "I knew they'd assumed I was either easy or stupid, because getting involved with you was..."

"Stupid?" he asked, voice and eyes hard.

"Frowned upon," she continued. "But I needed to know if I was pregnant more than I could afford to care what the marshals thought. Clara was the only one of my armed guards unafraid of making the purchase. She waited outside the bathroom door while I went in to see the results, and she held me up every step of the way afterward."

Blaze worked his jaw, eyes tight. "I'm glad you had someone there for you."

"Me, too."

"Have you had any issues with the pregnancy? Are you getting good prenatal care?" he asked.

Maisy nodded. "The best. I've got an OB in Myersville who's amazing. She understands my situation fully and has been a blessing to me and to our baby."

Blaze's pressed lips parted, and he pulled in a little breath.

Maisy gave herself a big mental push, then forged ahead with the speech she'd practiced a thousand times in her head, in the shower, in her sleep. "I know this is strange for you. I remember how shocked I was when I found out about the pregnancy, but I've had months to get my head around it, and since it's happening inside my body, I've had a constant reminder. But this has been completely sprung on you. I knew the minute I saw the little pink plus sign that I wanted to have this child. It's okay if you don't. You should take as long as you want to decide. I don't expect anything from you. And I'm fully prepared to raise our baby on my own, if that's what you choose. Though I could definitely use your help staying alive until Luciano is in prison," she improvised.

No matter how many times she'd planned to tell Blaze he could choose his level of involvement, none of those scenarios happened while she was on the run. "I can walk away after that, if you'd like," she continued, "but even then, my door will always be open for your visits, if you change your mind. Because, bottom line, Blaze. This is your baby, too. He or she is as much a part of you as me, and while I want our child to know you, and see what an amazing man you are, that will be up to you." She exhaled deeply, satisfied to have said the bulk of what she'd planned, if not quite as eloquently as she'd hoped.

Blaze blinked, then rubbed a heavy hand over his face.

"But those are conversations for another time," she said, pressing on. "Right now, we should probably figure out who's trying to kill me, and shut that down, so I make it to the trial."

BLAZE STARED ACROSS the table, mind reeling. He'd waited months to see Maisy's face again. Dreamed of it. Longed for it. But he'd never imagined she'd be pregnant when that day came. And now that she was, how could she consider for a second that he wouldn't take 100 percent responsibility for his child? Did she really think he wouldn't be all in for his kid? Did she not understand him at all?

He ground his teeth, keeping the emotions

in check. She was right about one thing. They could talk about this later, after he was sure she and his baby were safe. The threat against them was real and present. They had the rest of their—hopefully long—lives to celebrate the unexpected gift. Right now, he needed a plan.

Maisy raised an eyebrow. "You doing okay over there?"

"Never better."

She laughed, and his chest tightened. Maisy was just so damn beautiful. He'd forgotten the extent of it. Thick red hair, luminous hazel eyes. Porcelain skin and full pink lips. She'd stolen his breath at first sight, but he'd quickly learned not to let her beauty fool him. Maisy was smart, fast on her feet and fierce. She'd been formidable and single-minded in her quest to help locate Luciano all those months ago, and none of that had changed. The expression *whiskey in a teacup* had always come to mind when he thought of her. Sheer tenacity. Hell or high water. Packed in an incredibly distracting disguise. Even sitting here, in her last trimester of an unexpected pregnancy, with others being killed around her, she was still determined to see the criminal punished. Maisy would do whatever it took to honor the lives Luciano stole. There wasn't likely any stopping her, so he got on board.

"I've been thinking about the missing marshal," she said, as if on cue. "I saw the man who shot Clara. I think you should take me to the station and let me work with a sketch artist to get his image down. Then at least you'll know who you're looking for."

Blaze nodded. "I can use the image to find out if he's actually a marshal." Whoever the shooter was, he belonged behind bars, but if he was a US marshal, things would get a lot worse for Maisy fast. Marshals had access to files and details a typical criminal wouldn't, no matter how networked he or she was. And a marshal had something even more dangerous—the trust of other lawmen.

"Right," Maisy agreed. "Once we get a name to go with the face, we can track him down and stop him before he hurts any more witnesses."

Blaze leaned forward, pressing his forearms to the table and leveling her with his most intimidating expression. "Why don't we compromise," he suggested. "You describe him to me, then I'll meet with the sketch artist. The best thing you can do right now is lie low and let me handle this." He laced each word with heavy caution. A tone that had scared more than a few local thugs and gangsters. A tone he hoped would convey the importance of her going along with his request.

Maisy curled a thin, protective arm over her rounded middle, hazel eyes flashing in response. "Not a chance."

Chapter Five ·

Blaze dialed Sergeant Maxwell while Maisy cleaned up after breakfast. She'd insisted on splitting the duties. He'd made the meal, so she'd cleared the table, then refused his help washing dishes.

The call connected, and Blaze cleared his throat before leaving a message. "Hey, Sarge," he began, watching Maisy from across the room. "This is Blaze. I'm working in the field this morning, trying to make some progress on that task you gave me last night. Nothing so far, but I've got a few ideas I hope will pan out. I'll check in as information becomes available. I've got my phone on me if you need to reach me, or if you learn anything new I can work with." He disconnected, then ran a hand through his hair, hoping to hell his sergeant would recognize Blaze's intentional lack of details as a need to speak in person.

Maisy looked over her shoulder as she set

the final plate into the drying rack. "That was a pointedly vague message."

"I can't be sure who's listening." Blaze tucked the phone into his pocket. "Sergeant Maxwell asked me to find you and figure out what happened. He knows that will take time, so we've got some leeway to work with. He won't expect to see me around the office for a day or two."

"But I want to go in," she said, turning her back to the sink, and fixing her full attention on Blaze. "I want to talk with a sketch artist."

Blaze grinned at the wet line across her abdomen.

"Don't laugh," she said, curving loving arms around her bump and hiding the wet spot. "It's not as easy to reach things as it used to be. I practically have to climb onto the counter just to turn on the faucet."

He shook his head. "Don't move. I'll be right back." He strode into his laundry area, amused, among other things, by Maisy's growing middle. He pulled her clothes from the dryer and shook the pieces out.

"What are you doing?" she asked.

He turned slowly to smile at her. He hadn't heard her following him, though he should have expected as much. "You're stealthy."

"For someone my size?" she asked, curling thin fingers over newly rounded hips.

"Just stealthy," he corrected. "For anyone."

"Smart answer," she teased. "But, really, what are you doing? We were talking."

Blaze handed her the outfit. "I found these in my bathroom and washed them. I thought you'd want your own clothes to go out in today."

Maisy stared at the maternity shirt, pants and underthings she'd arrived in. A pretty blush spread across her ivory skin. "You washed my clothes?"

"I assumed you wouldn't want to go anywhere in my sweatpants and hoodie."

She accepted the offering, and Blaze stuffed his fingers into his jeans pockets. "Thank you."

"You're welcome."

Maisy nodded, eyes glistening with emotion as she raised the outfit to her nose and inhaled. "Care if I hit the shower?"

"Go for it."

"Then we'll go see the sketch artist?" she asked.

He laughed. There was no sidetracking her. That hadn't changed. "I need to make a few calls to coordinate your visit, but once I know I can keep you safe there, we'll go."

"Okay," Maisy agreed. "Thank you." She turned to leave, and Blaze caught her elbow.

"Hey." A jolt of electricity shot through him as their nearness registered, stirring emotions he thought he'd tucked neatly away. "One more thing before you shower. I have something on my desk I think you should keep." He stepped into the hall, releasing her when he wanted to pull her against him.

Maisy followed silently across the open space outside the laundry room.

He lifted the department-issued Taser and held it between them. "I pulled it from my gun safe this morning. It's charged and ready. I want you to keep it on you at all times."

She reached for the device tentatively. "You want me to use a Taser on someone?"

"Yes." He nodded, widening his stance and crossing his arms. "And I want you to respond immediately. Don't waste time thinking. Trust your instincts, release the safety, here, then press the trigger. Here." He pointed to each feature as he spoke. "Feel threatened? Pull trigger. Got it? I don't even care if you accidentally tase a harmless citizen. I'll make the necessary apologies later." He put his hand over hers and fixed her with a pointed stare. "I'd rather you zap a dozen innocent men than hesitate and not zap a killer."

Maisy raised her brows. "I'm not sure how I feel about all that, but I promise to act in the spirit of your request."

"I accept. But I meant what I said. Better safe than sorry."

She rolled her eyes. "Sure. As long as you're not one of the innocent people I zap."

He frowned. "Should we give it a practice run?"

"I think I've got it. Now, I'll take a shower so we can get started on this day and hopefully figure out where the man who killed Clara is now. He's our link to Luciano."

Blaze's gaze lowered to Maisy's distracting new curves at the mention of her in the shower.

"Call the sketch artist," she said, then disappeared with her clothes and the Taser.

Blaze took a moment to enjoy the sweet tension in his muscles as she walked away. He couldn't be sure what Maisy thought of her new figure, but the fact she carried his baby was unequivocally the hottest thing he'd ever known.

He gave a soft whistle, then liberated his phone and dialed Sarah at the station.

When Maisy emerged from the bathroom, she looked like something off a billboard. Her tousled, towel-dried hair hung down her back in auburn waves. Her skin was pink from the steamy shower, and her lips shone with what he guessed to be a layer of her old lip gloss. One he was intimately familiar with. One that tasted like his best memories.

"Did you make the appointment?" she asked.

"Four o'clock," he said. "She normally leaves at three, but she was booked all day, and I didn't want to wait until tomorrow. I told her this was a special circumstance situation, and that I needed her to keep the appointment under wraps. She agreed and fit us in at the end of the day."

Maisy tugged the hem of her tunic top. "Thank you. For everything."

"Whatever you need," he said, flashing a wicked smile. "West Liberty's finest. At your service."

"I hoped you'd say that."

Blaze mentally skated backward over his words, half-afraid to ask. "Why?"

"I appreciate you washing my clothes, but I can't keep wearing this same outfit every day," she said. "I need the rest of my things from the safe house. I thought we could make a trip over there today. Now we have time before seeing the sketch artist."

Blaze checked his watch, then gave Maisy and her rounded middle a long look. "The house is probably sealed as a crime scene," he said, working through the possibility of liberating her wardrobe. "If the house wasn't fully processed yesterday, we could run into a forensics team. And even if the place is empty, and we can get in, Luciano could have someone watching. Either for your return, or to pick up leads from visiting law enforcement."

She chewed her lip, easily drawing his attention there. "I had to leave everything when I ran. It'd be really nice to have more of my things. My mom's book is still there. Photographs of Natalie and me."

Blaze teetered, weighing the options. The maternity clothes were something he could replace. Her personal keepsakes were not. He sighed, recognizing defeat as it registered. Protecting and pleasing Maisy didn't always line up, and this was a prime example of one of those times. But he knew what her mother's book meant to her. Her sister had unintentionally died retrieving it. Losing the treasure to Luciano now seemed wrong. "I'll agree to a drive-by only. If we see any activity at the house or anyone loitering in a car nearby, we leave."

"Deal."

MAISY CLIMBED INTO Blaze's truck, wearing his gray hooded sweatshirt and black motorcycle jacket over her maternity shirt. Every strand of her long hair was tucked carefully inside a ball cap.

"Ready?" he asked, grinning as she grappled with her seat belt.

It wasn't easy to fit the safety measure below her bump and across her hips where it belonged, or guide it properly across her chest these days. The bulky layered coats didn't help. "Stop smiling," she said, laughing at the ridiculousness of her shape and seat belt predicament.

A sharp pain stilled her hands and twisted her expression into a grimace. She fastened the seat belt, then rubbed the alien-looking bulge on her abdomen. A tiny elbow, knee or foot had rammed against her ribs, temporarily stealing her breath.

"What's wrong?" Blaze asked, panic flashing in his dark eyes.

She exhaled as the infant moved again. "It's okay. The baby is running out of room and likes to use my organs as a trampoline park."

Blaze cringed, then started the truck with a nervous laugh. "Maybe it's better that I haven't been around. I'd probably have raced you to the hospital a dozen times by now."

Maisy watched as he shifted into gear and headed down the driveway. "It's not better," she said softly. She would've gladly made those unnecessary trips if it'd meant having him around.

Pleasure twinkled in his eyes as they turned onto the road.

"I was afraid, too, at first," she said, dragging her gaze back to the road. "Dr. Nazir has been great. She gave me her personal number, and I called her a lot those first few months." Maisy chuckled. "I was terrified something would go wrong, but she told me which symptoms to watch out for and what was considered normal. She advised on everything from diet and exercise to sleep positions and my birth plan. Basically, she's held my hand every step of the way. Clara, too. Clara has kids of her own, so she…" Maisy froze. "Had," she corrected. "Clara *had* kids of her own." But now those kids were orphans so Maisy's baby wouldn't be.

"Hey." Blaze set a broad palm over her hand on the seat between them. "This isn't your fault. None of it. We've talked about this. Remember?"

She tried to force a smile but failed. Blaze had spent countless moments in the months she'd shared with him assuring her the only person to blame was Luciano. On the whole, she knew it was true, but deep down, she couldn't help acknowledging that Natalie and Clara would be alive if it wasn't for her. So, maybe Aaron's death was all on Luciano, but Maisy's sister and her assigned marshal were only in his path because of her.

Blaze stole glances at her as he drove, maybe waiting for her to respond, but she couldn't. "I'm sorry I've missed your pregnancy," he said, flicking his gaze briefly to her bump. "I would've been there. Every step. If I could've."

She smiled, a genuine feeling of warmth spreading through her. "I know."

She'd prepared herself for the worst when she told him he could walk away last night, but it would've surprised her if he had. Family meant everything to the Winchesters, especially Blaze. That's just who he was. Whether or not he still wanted her was another story, but they had bigger things to figure out first. Like where Clara's killer went, and if he knew Maisy was with Blaze. As for a future with the father of her child, Maisy didn't expect him to want that. Their romance had been based on heightened emotions and circumstances. And any foundation built on sex, especially when she was currently the size of a barn, was sure to collapse.

"Have you heard the baby's heartbeat?"

Blaze asked, drawing her attention back to the moment.

"Sure. At every visit for the last few months." She chewed her lip, collecting her nerve. "I see Dr. Nazir every two weeks now. My next appointment is in a few days. If you'd like to come, you can stay with me during the exam." Maisy had talked to the doctor about Blaze an embarrassing amount, but she could hardly help herself. Blaze had come to represent her old life, her freedom and a time when she'd never felt more cherished. "I know she'd like to meet you."

His lips parted, and his eyes widened. "Yes. Please. I'd like that. Very much."

"Okay." She nodded, fighting a too-broad smile. "Good, but you should probably lower your expectations. The appointments aren't as exciting as you might think."

"I doubt that." Blaze squeezed her hand. "Thank you."

The drive to the next county passed in a mix of electric energy and companionable silence. The butterflies in Maisy's stomach gave her acrobatic baby some real competition for room and overall flutters.

The turn onto her old street, and the appearance of her temporary home erased all the good feelings in the space of a heartbeat.

Her eyes stung with grief and heartbreak.

Blaze released her hand, curling long, steady fingers around the steering wheel instead. "Let's make another pass or two before we stop."

She stared in silence as they rolled past the familiar driveway. The small white cottage with its pale blue shutters and cheery yellow door twisted her heart painfully. She imagined Clara planting perennials in the spring. Beautiful things to look forward to, she'd claimed. Because everyone needed those. She'd been sure the symbolism matched perfectly with Maisy's situation. She only had to plant some seeds of hope and dream of new beginnings. When she emerged from protective custody, the worst would be behind her. She'd have a new baby and a beautiful new beginning.

Oxygen seemed to rush from her lungs as an onslaught of uglier, more recent memories overtook her. Too raw and too recent to manage.

Blaze eased his truck into the driveway several minutes later, then settled the engine. "You okay?"

"Nervous," she admitted, casting a quick glance his way. "The last time I was here, someone came to kill me."

Blaze scanned the scene beyond the window.

"Well, let's get in and out. No reason to hang around in case that guy comes back."

She blew out a steady breath, then reached for her door handle.

"At least the shooter didn't get a look at you. The image shared on the news was from last year. Your hair was shorter and straightened in the photo. You had bangs, and you weren't pregnant."

"Well, thank you for this shapely disguise," she said, setting her hands on the enormous bump with an awkward smile. "Honestly, I barely recognize myself half the time, so I guess you're right. It would be hard to pick me out from an old photo."

Blaze nodded, then climbed down from the cab, his blank cop expression in place. He rounded the truck's hood and met her on her side, offering her a hand when she opened the door.

They moved to the home's front door in tandem, then paused at the broken crime scene seal on the door.

Blaze pulled his gun from the holster, looked at Maisy and frowned.

"I'm not staying out here alone," she said. "If that's what you're thinking. No way."

Blaze pressed his lips tight, weighing the options. He swore under his breath, then turned his back to her and placed one of her hands on his lean, sculpted side. "Stay close. Consider me your shield."

He opened the door, and they entered the small cottage together, navigating the space. Blaze cleared each room as unbidden tears rolled over Maisy's cheeks. Bloodstains marred the living room walls and carpet where she'd last seen Clara, gun drawn and calling for backup. Everything in sight had been over-turned, dumped or destroyed.

"Why would they do this?" Maisy asked. "What evidence can be found by tearing a home apart?"

"This isn't the work of a crime scene team," Blaze said, putting his gun away. "Someone came in when they left. Whoever did this broke the seal on the door and then, apparently, searched for something."

"Like what?" Maisy shivered at the thought of strangers ripping through her things, pawing at her little cottage life.

Blaze fixed her with an icy stare. "You."

Chapter Six

Blaze loaded Maisy's belongings into the bed of his pickup truck. Three lidded plastic totes. Two duffel bags and a few boxes of books. The entire contents of what was left of her life amounted to less, materially, than his personal collection of fishing gear.

She'd given up everything in her quest to find justice for Luciano's victims, and it both filled and pained Blaze's heart. He needed to make sure she got the chance to complete her mission.

He pulled a heavy tarp over her things and secured it, then joined her in the cab. "You okay?" he asked. He couldn't imagine how tough it must've been, seeing the place again so soon, especially in that condition. Her expression as she'd packed had said plenty. She was angry and afraid, but more than that, Maisy was tired. It was written on her face, but she was too darn stubborn to admit it or lean on him for support. He just didn't understand why.

"Not going to lie," she said. "Being here wasn't great." Her voice shook as she spoke, and Blaze longed to fold her into his arms.

Instead, he started the engine and shifted immediately into gear, getting out of there as quickly as possible. In case whoever tossed the place returned.

"I'm glad to have my stuff back, but I'd hoped to find some kind of clue that would help us track the killer. Instead the whole cottage was trashed and the trip was a 50 percent bust."

Blaze turned to her as she stared dejectedly through the window. "The crime scene tape was broken, so we can assume officials had already done their job before it was overturned. Most likely, whatever clues the shooter left behind were already collected before the home was sealed."

"Maybe," she muttered. "Hopefully that wasn't done by a member of the crime scene to destroy or cover up the evidence."

Blaze tried to smile or muster any level of encouraging expression and failed miserably. He couldn't blame Maisy for her lack of faith in the system. Not when a man dressed as a marshal had killed her friend and guardian. It wasn't fair that she'd been through so much. Had given up so much. And he hated that she was only six weeks from delivering her first child, and she only had one tiny box of baby things. She should have a whole nursery set up by now, and a closet full of clothes. The pregnancy should've been celebrated, not hidden, and his family should have smothered her with love and attention so she could laugh about it with him each night. Maisy and their baby should be safe. Not on the run.

His grip tightened on the steering wheel.

"I'm fine, Blaze," she said, drawing his attention to her. "I hate that look, so do me a favor and don't use it on me."

"What look?" he asked, straightening his spine and doing his best impression of someone handling the situation better than he was. "I was thinking. That's all."

"You were thinking that you pity me," she said, "And I don't want it. So, knock it off."

He bit the insides of his cheeks, fighting the urge to argue and knowing she wouldn't listen anyway. They'd both get all wound up, throwing their misplaced frustrations and anger at one another until someone said something they didn't mean and couldn't take back. They'd both regret their parts immediately and miserably afterward. He and Maisy had had a few of those explosive debates in their hey-day. Each had ended in explosive makeup sex and hours of profuse apologies. The possibility of makeup sex was clearly out of the question. He'd be lucky if Maisy ever let him touch her again after he'd gotten her pregnant and left her alone for half a year. He definitely couldn't argue with her right now. He had enough regrets already and wasn't in the market for more.

She kept her attention focused through the window at her side, stroking her bump, comforting the child inside her.

Blaze longed to do the same. Wanted to caress the place where his baby grew and touch the woman who'd once stolen his heart. A woman who'd yet to give it back. But he kept his hands to himself, certain she thought he'd touched her enough already. "It's empathy," he said, finally, unable to let her think he pitied her. "I'm saddened by what you're going through because I care about your happiness, and I think it sucks that you're stuck in this psychopath's storm. You gave up everything because of him, including your freedom. For months. And now that you've made it to the finish line, he's pulled the rug and set you back at the beginning. On the run all over again.

Scared. Unsure who to trust. I don't pity you, Maze. I'm angry for you."

She turned heated hazel eyes on him. "I know who I can trust. You. And I know you'll get me through this, whatever it takes. You'll keep me safe until I can do what I set out to do. Be the voice that Natalie, Clara and all Luciano's other victims no longer have."

The return drive passed in a flash of trees and small-town blurs outside his window. Maisy was quiet until a dime store appeared in the distance just outside the West Liberty city limits. "Do you think they have a restroom?" she asked. "I could use a break, and probably a bottle of water."

"It's worth a try if you need one," he said, pulling the truck into a long, narrow lot, glad for the opportunity to meet at least one of her needs. If the business didn't have a public restroom, he'd use his badge to temporarily change the policy.

He snagged a spot near the door and gave the place a long, careful look. The building was large, some sort of renovated warehouse or repurposed pole barn, not uncommon outside the city limits. A vinyl sign hung from the rooftop with the words *Now Open* scripted in red.

He scanned the area carefully before unlocking the truck doors and heading around to help Maisy down from the cab.

Thankfully, the ladies' room was clearly marked at the back of the building, and Blaze didn't have to pull rank on a retail worker. On the off chance anyone stopped here to ask about Maisy, it wouldn't be good for employees to remember she'd been with him.

Blaze lingered outside the closed restroom door, an aisle of baby things stretching before him. A smattering of shoppers perused the selections. Blaze's feet pulled him forward without conscious intent, into the foreign, brightly colored world. Images of happy children stared back from every baby-based product imaginable, and many he'd never imagined. The brands, sizes and options in diapers and formula were infinite and intimidating. There was a section of special laundry soaps, medicines with droppers and little silicon finger puppet–style toothbrushes for cleaning babies' gums.

His gut tightened, and his skin prickled with fear and enthusiasm. This was his future. All these things he'd never seen before were about to become his everyday normal. A growing bud of panic gave way to an unexpected rush of joy as that beautiful truth settled in. He was going to be a father.

In six weeks.

He read labels and dragged his fingertips across lace bonnets and terry-cloth bibs. Tiny shirts with adorable sayings like *Daddy's Little Princess* had images of shiny crowns. Blue overalls with cartoon chicks were embroidered with the words *Chick Magnet*. It was all too tiny and cute. There were booties printed to look like athletic shoes and cowboy boots.

He wanted to buy it all.

"First time?" a man asked, both startling and horrifying Blaze.

He blinked unfocused eyes, shocked that he'd allowed a stranger to get so close without him knowing. "Sorry. What?" He smiled apologetically as he assessed the man. Harmless. Young. His unbuttoned uniform shirt tagged him as a local mechanic.

The guy grinned. "New dad?" he asked. "You've got that look. I'm on number four. I can help you choose a diaper. How old's your kid?"

Blaze shook his head. "No, not yet. Thank you."

The man puckered his brows.

"Excuse me." Blaze rushed back to the restrooms, unsure how long he'd been in the aisle, lost in thought.

The ladies' room door was open when he arrived. The single-occupant unit empty.

A flood of panic ripped through him. "Maisy?" he said, turning to scan the store in search of her wild red curls. "Maisy?" He hurried along the rear wall, peering down each aisle into the faces of strangers. "Maisy!"

"Blaze?"

He spun in place, heart hammering painfully against his ribs.

Maisy waved tentatively back from several feet away. He hadn't recognized her, dressed in his bulky jackets, her hair stuffed into his ball cap.

Relief hit like a baseball bat as he closed the distance between them and wrapped his arms around her.

"Are you okay?" she asked, hugging him loosely, and with only one arm.

He laughed, embarrassed as he stepped back and scrubbed a hand over his mouth.

"You look a little bewildered." She frowned awkwardly, a crooked smile on her lips.

"I'm fine," he said. Hooking a hand on his hip and pulling himself together. "Where were you?"

"Shopping. I thought I should change my look, so I don't have to masquerade as a pregnant man until the trial ends." She dragged a palm over his motorcycle jacket in illustration.

"Right." Blaze peeked into the plastic shopping basket in her grip. Hair dye, makeup and glasses cluttered the bottom of the little carrier. "Sounds like a plan. May I?" He tugged the thin metal handles, and Maisy released the basket.

She slipped her arm around his as they made their way to the checkout counter. "Thanks. I could've carried it myself, but I appreciate the gesture."

His racing heart settled easily under her touch. "How about we agree you're as strong as an ox, but I'll do the lifting anyway for the next six weeks? It'll make me feel useful."

"Only if you never compare me to an ox again."

"Y'all find everything all right?" a portly middle-aged woman asked from behind the counter. She wore a blue vest with the store logo and half glasses over small brown eyes. A name badge identified her as Theresa.

"Yes, thank you," Maisy said, releasing Blaze in favor of winding both arms over her bump.

Blaze set the basket on the counter.

"When are you due?" Theresa asked, cheerfully scanning the selections. "Boy or girl?"

"Soon," Maisy said. "We're keeping the gender a surprise."

The clerk's eyes widened, and she belted out

a laugh. "Well, I don't hear that much these days. Folks like to plan every little second of their lives. Good for you. Enjoying the moments as they come." She totaled the bill and dropped the final item into a bag.

Blaze offered her a few bills and waited for change.

"Well, good luck with everything," she said. "You sure are one nice-looking family. Bring that baby back around here when I can meet it."

"Will do," Blaze promised, chest puffing with pride as he lifted the bags and led Maisy back to the truck.

MAISY SET THE blow-dryer onto Blaze's bathroom countertop and stared at the reflection before her. Gone were the long red curls. Present was a blunt, poker-straight, shoulder-length bob with heavy bangs in a deep mocha brown she hated. She'd followed the guidance of an online makeup tutorial to generate a dramatic smoky-eye look and enhance her cheekbones. Her full pink lips were painted in matte crimson instead of the neutral gloss she'd used since high school.

"I look like a pregnant hooker," she told the alternate version of herself looking back at her through cat-eye glasses. Then she pressed the tip of an eyebrow pencil into the skin near her upper lip. "Right down to the fake beauty mark."

Thankfully, she still had her own clothes. A simple, long-sleeved red T-shirt and maternity jeans.

"Maze?" Blaze called, rapping softly on the semiopen door.

"Nope." She turned to wait as Blaze peeked inside. "There's no one by that name in here."

His lips parted as he stepped into the threshold and leaned against the doorjamb. "Whoa."

"Yeah." She turned back to the mirror. "At least Luciano's henchmen won't recognize me. I barely recognize myself."

Blaze locked eyes with her reflection. "You look like a hot librarian. Or a naughty schoolteacher."

Maisy turned to face him, dragging the glasses to the tip of her nose. "Well then, how about a ride to the station before I give you detention?"

Blaze flashed a wicked grin before peeling himself away from the jamb. "Yes, ma'am."

THE POLICE STATION was busy as they made their way to an office near the back.

A pretty blonde with blue eyes and graphite-smudged fingers popped up to greet them.

"Detective Winchester." She reached for Blaze, eagerly shaking his hand, before turning her attention to Maisy. "I'm Sarah. It's lovely to meet you."

"Hi," she answered, reluctant to share her name. "Thank you for agreeing to meet me on such short notice. I understand you usually go home by now."

"It's no problem," Sarah assured. "I'm glad to help. Have a seat."

Maisy sat opposite Sarah and rested her hands on the table.

Sarah stared openly a moment before blushing. "Sorry," she said, looking immeasurably guilty. "It's just that you don't look anything like the picture on the news. I hope you don't mind. Lucas filled me in."

Maisy looked to Blaze, hoping his brother knew what he was doing by sharing her identity with the sketch artist.

Blaze offered a nearly imperceptible nod.

"Well, that was the goal," Maisy said, answering the woman's comment about her appearance. "It's a little much, right?" She waved her hands in a small circle around her hair and face.

Sarah laughed. "You're obviously beautiful either way, but this is a great cover. The bump was a brilliant touch."

"The bump is real," Maisy said, wrapping her arms around her middle.

Sarah's brows rose. "Oh. Sorry. I didn't know."

"It's okay. Most don't."

"Well, congratulations?" Sarah offered.

Maisy grinned, feeling the warmth of her well-wishes spread through her.

Blaze rocked back on his heels. "Thank you." He set a hand on Maisy's shoulder, his thumb stroking the fabric of her jacket.

Sarah's jaw dropped. "No. You two? Really?"

Maisy laughed, a shock of pleasure and electricity coursing through her. "True story."

"Winchester!" A man's voice boomed outside the door.

Blaze pulled his hand away as if he'd been burned. "Sergeant," he returned, spinning toward the door.

Maisy twisted in her seat for a look through the open doorway, but she didn't recognize any of the faces outside.

"Will you two be okay without me?" Blaze asked, moving toward the door. "I want to brief Sergeant Maxwell on the situation and talk to the marshals if they're here."

Maisy smiled. "I'm sure we can manage on our own awhile."

"Go for it," Sarah said. "I'm going to need at least thirty minutes."

Blaze nodded, stepping into the hallway. He smiled at Maisy before pulling the door shut behind him.

"So the rumors are true," Sarah said, grinning as she lifted her pencil to the paper. "Blaze Winchester is officially off the market."

"Oh no." Maisy blanched. "It's not like that between us anymore. Until yesterday, I hadn't seen him since they took me into protective custody. He didn't even know about the baby until I showed up on his doorstep." She bit her lip, hating the unnecessary overshare. She cleared her throat and tried again. "Right now we're just... I don't know. Trying to stay alive, I guess." She laughed to alleviate the awkward moment she'd created, but only felt more uncomfortable.

Sarah leaned over her sketch pad, still waiting to make the first line. "I hate to break the news, but that man is clearly lost for you. I know you're in a tough place right now. A crazy crime boss is trying to kill you and all that, but I work with these guys all day. Every day. And that bright-eyed detective who just strode out of here isn't the same man I've watched mope and skulk around for the past six months. That guy right there—" she pointed to the door, as if Blaze was still visible through it "—he's a man who just found his way home."

Maisy's heart swelled nonsensically. She didn't know Sarah, or have a clue how well Sarah knew Blaze, but she really liked the woman's opinion. "I'll take your word for it," she said, hoping she was right.

"You can take it to the bank," she said. "Now, what do you say we get the safe house shooter's face all over the news and shut Luciano down?"

Maisy beamed. Exactly what she was there for.

She and Sarah worked diligently until the sketch of Clara's shooter was nearly perfect. Maisy marveled at the way Sarah's hand moved confidently over the page, adding lines and curves, then dragging skilled fingertips across the work, blending to create depth, shade and shadow. The result was remarkable and could easily be mistaken for a black-and-white photograph.

Maisy's abdomen tightened unexpectedly, and she grunted in response to the sudden pain.

"Maisy?" Sarah asked, eyes wide with instant concern.

"False contractions," she answered softly, puffing short, labored breaths. She stretched onto her feet as the pain subsided, then paced the small room in slow, even strides, smoothing her palms against the hardened sides of her middle. "Sorry. I'll just walk it off."

Sarah offered an understanding smile. "Braxton-Hicks can be the worst," she said. "So painful and such a tease. You'll be praying for the real thing in a month or so, and these jokers will get your hopes up for nothing."

Maisy laughed. "I can't wait for that." Praying for labor would mean the trial was over and she'd survived.

Another sharp pain cut the relief short, and Maisy gritted her teeth.

"Do you need a break?" Sarah asked. "There's a restroom in a little alcove a few doors down from here. A water fountain and snack machines, too. Across from Detective Winchester's office. Out this door and to the left. You can't miss it. Go stretch and breathe."

Maisy bobbed her head, inhaling long and slow through her nose as she straightened her spine. She released the air through open lips. "Okay. I won't be long." She hooked her purse over her shoulder, then gritted her way through another punch of pain.

"I'll finish up, then come and check on you," Sarah promised. "Remember, go left. Right is the way back to the main lobby, and the door will lock behind you if you leave."

Maisy turned left, then checked over her shoulder to be sure there wasn't any miscommunication amid the pain.

Sarah gave a thumbs-up, and Maisy shuffled away, eyes locked on a blue-and-white sign identifying the restrooms and vending area.

Blaze's office door was open, but the room was empty.

The hall ended in a bullpen of sorts, lined in desks and filled with people in uniforms, suits and street clothes. Voices rose into a cloud of noise, punctuated with ringing phones and the click-clack of a dozen hands on keyboards. She suppressed the pinch of fear rising in her. Everyone in sight appeared to be official in one way or another. Even a man dressed as a homeless person had a badge on a chain around his neck.

You're safe, she told herself as she hurried into the ladies' room, cringing and breathing like a lunatic.

She jammed a wad of paper towels under running water, then squeezed out the excess before pressing the cool compress to her forehead. She wiped her temples, then repeated the process, holding the towels against the back of her neck.

The door to the bathroom opened, and

Maisy bowed her head farther, balancing the towels and avoiding eye contact.

The scent of men's cologne sprang her upright.

"No." Terror choked the word as she looked Clara's shooter in the eye.

He grabbed her in one swift move, pulling her to him with powerful arms. A broad, leather-gloved hand clamped over her lips, and he lowered his mouth to her ear. "We're walking out of here," he whispered. "And you aren't going to fight me on it, or I will hurt your baby. Got it?"

Maisy sucked in a ragged breath, nodding wildly and fumbling for her purse.

The man's icy blue eyes met hers in the mirror, and she stilled as her fingers reached their goal. "Think of that baby," he said, the words filled with warning and resolve. "Don't be a hero."

He turned her toward the restroom's exit with a forceful jerk, then shoved her forward. "Down the hall and to the right. We're leaving through the back door."

Maisy whimpered, then groaned, bending slightly forward with the sound.

When he attempted to wrench her upright, she pulled the Taser from her purse and pressed the trigger.

Chapter Seven

Blaze scanned the space outside his sergeant's office; the normally busy area was borderline chaos. Officers, detectives and a collection of men and women far above his pay grade filled every nook, corner and cranny. The entire county population of law enforcement seemed to be on hand, plotting, planning and conspiring to get a location on Maisy, the missing witness, and her marshal. Thankfully, Blaze had Lucas on board to run interference as needed, and a sergeant who'd protect Maisy with his life, once Blaze had the chance to fill him in.

Getting Maxwell alone, long enough to bring him up to speed, however, wouldn't be easy. Even members of administration and guards from the jail where Luciano was being held had shown up to make sense of what was happening and to form a collaboration to stop him. Thanks to Luciano's long list of crimes and extensive network, every agency from the

IRS to the FBI had a dog in the fight. And every agency wanted to be the one who broke the case.

Sergeant Maxwell pressed his palms against the desk, leveling a pair of local marshals with his most resolute stare. "I appreciate your determination to take the Luciano situation off our hands here, but Maisy Daniels is our witness. She's a West Liberty citizen who worked in direct cooperation with Detective Winchester for four months when Luciano went underground. She's the reason there will even be a trial. That young woman lost her twin sister to that piece of garbage. She willingly gave up her freedom in exchange for the marshals' protection and a chance to testify against him."

The marshals narrowed their eyes in defiance, knowing Maxwell was right but not wanting to take full responsibility for what had happened at the safe house. "How could we have known something like this would happen?"

"Because it's your job to know," Maxwell retorted. "You botched her protection. Now I'm ready to accept whatever help we can get to assure she's found and protected until she can do what she set out to do, which is make your case for you."

The marshal smirked, hands clasped before him. "Thanks, but we've got this covered."

Maxwell's face went from an irritated red to a ready-to-explode purple. "She trusted us, and we trusted you. Now a marshal is dead, and our witness is missing days before the trial. Not to mention the other witnesses are dropping like flies. So, you'll excuse me if I want all hands on deck. That means my men are on this, and staying on it."

The marshal in charge glared, deep-set brown eyes flashing. "I'm sure you mean well, Sergeant, but watch your step here. It sounds as if you're making unwarranted accusations about our abilities to perform our jobs, or worse, that we have a dirty marshal. I won't stand here and put up with that. What happened at that safe house was a tragedy, but it wasn't something anyone could've prepared for. Including you, so I suggest you stop glowering and pointing fingers."

Blaze bit his tongue, knowing more than he could share. That Maisy had confirmed the missing marshal from the news wasn't the man who'd shot Clara. The shooter had been an impostor, and the true marshal sent for her transport was likely dead. He checked his watch, eager for the marshals to leave so he could confide Maisy's appearance quietly to Maxwell and decide what to do from there. He'd already been away from her too long. Sarah had to be finishing the sketch by now.

A sharp scream pierced the white noise outside Maxwell's door, and the room fell silent for a lingering heartbeat.

Blaze's feet were in motion instantly, as if the scream had triggered his fight-or-flight system, and every fiber of his being already knew Maisy was the woman who'd screamed.

And he was ready to fight.

The thick collection of bodies in the busy central space parted as he ran toward the sound. Toward the restroom, he realized, not the office where he'd left her with Sarah.

Maisy appeared in the next second, pale and terrified, racing through the crowd, every member of which was suddenly on high alert. She collided with him, tears streaming, breaths coming short and fast. "I tased him!" she panted. "In the bathroom. The ladies' room. Clara's shooter."

Blaze didn't have to speak. Uniformed officers broke away without question, jogging toward the women's restroom as Blaze wrapped Maisy in his arms.

He caught Lucas's eye in the commotion as he led her to his office, only a few yards away.

She nearly collapsed onto the chair as Blaze

shut the door. She curled inward, rolling her shoulders over her bump and wrapping protective arms around it as she began to sob.

His muscles ached to hold her. And also to take care of whoever had dared lay a hand on her. "Hey. You're okay." He crouched on the floor before her chair, seeking her eyes with his. Fury and terror raced in his veins. However much he wanted to get ahold of the man who'd attacked her, Maisy needed him, and her needs would always trump his. Her happiness and safety were integral to his own. "You're safe now," he said softly. "Did he hurt you?"

She shook her head as she cried, dark eye makeup twisting black rivulets over bright red cheeks. "It was him, Blaze! The safe house shooter reached me here. At the police station. How long can I possibly stay alive if there's no place he can't get to me?"

"Hey." He raised his palms tentatively, cupping her jaw and brushing strands of freshly dyed brown locks away from her wet cheeks with his thumbs. "You'll survive as long as you have to because you are who you are," he said. "You're tough and you're resilient. And you're not going to let Luciano or one of his henchmen change that."

She lifted puffy eyes to his, her long lashes soaked with tears. "Okay."

"Good." He smiled. "Now, are you hurt?" he asked again. "Take a minute and think beyond the adrenaline. Is the baby okay? Do you need a medic?"

He gritted his teeth behind the smile, aching to tear in half the son of a gun who'd caused this. He scanned her pretty face, her neck, limbs and middle. She was too covered, long sleeves. Jeans. Dressed for the falling temperature outside. Even if he could confirm there were no scratches or bruises, how could he have any idea what kind of damage might've been done internally? This kind of stress couldn't be good for her or their baby.

"I'm not hurt," she said. "Shaken, but that's all." She rubbed her wrists, then ran shaky palms over her arms, presumably attempting to scrub away the effects of her attacker's touch. "He only had ahold of me for a second, thanks to your Taser."

Blaze pulled the cell phone from his pocket. "I'd feel better if Isaac took a look at you. We don't have to go to the hospital if he doesn't think it's necessary, but I don't want to take any chances. You remember Isaac? You liked him."

Isaac was the youngest Winchester, a fairer-skinned, lighter-haired, first-cousin, practically raised in Blaze's family home. They weren't brothers by birth, but they were un-equivocally brothers, and Blaze trusted Isaac's medical opinion more highly than any other medic's in the county.

Maisy gave a shaky nod. "I remember." Her bump seemed to move, and she settled a hand over the spot where Blaze had seen the small pulse point. "Okay," she said. "Thank you."

Blaze forced his eyes away from her middle, heart thundering for a new reason now. It was easy to think of the baby abstractly, like an idea more than reality, until he saw evidence of its movement. Its life. His throat thickened and his head filled with questions. Was she carrying a boy or a girl? His son? Or his daughter? "You did good, Maze," he said, barely choking back the emotion. "You protected yourself and the baby. All on your own. And I swear I won't ever make you do that again."

She reached a small hand out to him, gliding her palm against his cheek. "This isn't your fault. This is all Luciano, and we need to stop him."

Blaze covered her hand with his, then, winding long fingers around her narrow wrist, he pressed a kiss against the soft skin of her palm. "I was wrong to think any place was safe. I knew the guy impersonated a marshal. I should've known he could be anywhere, pose as anyone. Clearly, he has connections." The words led to another sobering thought. "Someone let him in here. And I'm going to find out who."

A heavy knock rattled the door, standing Blaze at attention, one hand on his gun and prepared to draw. "Blaze?" His brother's voice called from the hall outside.

He opened up and urged Lucas inside. "What'd you learn?"

Lucas glanced from Blaze to Maisy, then back. "The bathroom was empty, but we got him on the security feed, using the rear entrance for his escape. Tech's working backward now, watching to catch him coming in. My best guess is that someone left the door ajar for him, maybe with a stopper of some kind."

Maisy twisted on her seat, eyes wide. "So someone here is definitely dirty."

"Looks like," Lucas said. "Problem is, half the lawmen in the county are here. We've got marshals and jail personnel on top of our uniforms and detectives on-site right now. And assuming I'm right about the door being left ajar, who's to say the person who did that didn't leave the premises afterward? The dirty one might not even be here anymore."

Blaze groaned. "There's no camera pointed

at the door from the inside, either. Just from the lot."

"Maxwell's working with tech services," Lucas said. "He thinks the exterior camera could have picked up an image in the glass. We might still be able to find out who helped the guy get in here."

"Knock, knock," Sarah called from outside the door. "It's Sarah."

Lucas opened the door and pulled her inside. "Hey."

"Hey," she answered, her eyes darting to Maisy as she pushed onto her feet. "Oh thank goodness!" The women met in a hug.

"I'm okay," Maisy assured.

"I'm not," Sarah said, shaking her head. "I think I had a heart attack when I heard you scream. Then everyone was running around, and no one knew where you went."

Lucas's eyes widened at the sight of Maisy's round middle, which had been somewhat hidden until she stood and turned to face them.

Blaze grinned despite himself. Knowing she was pregnant and seeing the evidence were two different experiences. "How's the sketch?" he asked, changing the subject.

"Finished." Sarah turned the image around to show them.

Lucas pointed at the paper. "That's him. From the security footage."

Maisy nodded, going pale, then returning to her seat. "Yeah. He's the one who attacked the safe house."

Tension rippled through the room. Blaze shot a text to Isaac, requesting he stop by the station and take a look at Maisy, then returned his attention to her. "Isaac's on the way."

"Are you hurt?" Lucas asked, a thread of panic around the words.

"No, I'm fine," she assured. "We're just being cautious. Plus, I doubt Blaze would let me leave this office until I agreed to an exam."

Lucas edged closer, smile widening. "I don't blame him. You're carrying precious cargo, I hear."

Maisy laughed, hands going to her middle. "That's pretty obvious these days."

Lucas grinned. "You've undergone quite a makeover."

"Unfortunately," she said, pulling a wad of tissues from the box on Blaze's desk and running them over her makeup-drenched face. "I didn't fool that guy, whoever he is. Thankfully Blaze armed me with a Taser this morning."

"Where is it?" Lucas asked, voicing the words before Blaze could form them.

"I dropped it when I ran."

Nonsensical pride bubbled in Blaze's chest. She hadn't wanted to take the Taser, but she had, and she'd promised to use it in the spirit he'd intended. And she'd done a bang-up job.

Blaze's desk phone rang, and he nearly yanked it off the base, eager for an update. "Winchester."

"We're tracking the intruder through local surveillance cameras," Sergeant Maxwell said. "And we've collected a Taser from the floor of the women's restroom. Any idea why I'm calling you about that?"

Blaze waited.

"The weapon was department issued," he said. "To you. Got anything to say about it?"

Blaze looked to his brother before dragging his gaze to Maisy.

"I'll take your silence as a big fat yes, and trust you're going to fill me in on things as soon as you get Maisy Daniels to safety," Maxwell said. "I can only presume that's what's going on here, though I can't imagine why you'd bring her to the station considering our concerns about a leak at this level."

"You're absolutely right, sir. I intended to talk to you sooner, but the marshals—"

"Are a pain in my backside," he interrupted. "Fine. I'll stop by your office for an update as soon as I can. If you need to leave before I can get there, do it. Meanwhile, there's something more you should know."

Blaze froze, and his breath seemed to stop as he waited for the update.

"There's something I didn't get the chance to tell you earlier, too." Maxwell released a heavy sigh against the receiver. "We lost another witness on the Luciano case early this morning. That makes two in two days. And two consecutive attempts on Miss Daniels, as well. We're down to her and one other witness. Without them, Luciano's lawyers won't have any trouble getting him off these charges, per their usual. So, however you came to be back in touch with Maisy Daniels, you've got my permission to do whatever you need to keep her safe. Time off. Airfare to the moon. You got it. Just protect her."

"With my life, sir."

Chapter Eight

Maisy eased onto Blaze's couch, exhausted by the emotionally depleting day. From their visit to the safe house, where the memories and destruction had pushed her to request a bathroom break halfway home. So she could stand in a public restroom and cry. To her direct attack at the police station, where the psychopath who'd killed Clara had threatened her baby. It was all just too much, and she was certain she could sleep until her due date if the universe would let her.

Though, given her string of awful luck, she'd be happy with a thirty-minute power nap.

Thankfully, the police, marshals service and public at large had a face to go with the attacks now, and the man would be on the run. Unlikely to come for her again. Though that didn't mean another of Luciano's henchmen weren't on their way.

Blaze clattered around in the kitchen, cleaning up after a wonderful meal of steaks and baked potatoes. He'd insisted she rest instead of help, and she hadn't had the energy to protest.

She turned the television to the local news and let her eyelids slip shut, attempting to center herself in the moment and trust that she was safe again for now. The pair of Tylenol Isaac had recommended during her exam had taken the edge off her sore muscles, mostly aching from the tension she'd carried there for too long. Isaac had further prescribed plenty of rest, water and time off her feet. She'd always liked him.

"All right," Blaze said, sweeping into the room and heading for the couch. "What are you watching?"

"News," she said, as if anything else was an option for them. "Maybe the police captured the lunatic assigned to kill me and no one has bothered to call and tell you."

Blaze tented his brows. "That would be a serious inside scoop." He lifted her feet off the little cushion she'd propped them on, then tossed the pillow aside, easily taking its place. "Is this okay?" he asked, resting her ankles across his lap.

"I can sit up," she offered, squirming to attempt the task.

"No way." He gripped her calves gently, urging her to be still. "You were comfortable, and I interrupted."

"But it's rude of me to take up your whole couch," she countered.

"Let's compromise. You can have the couch back, and I'll put the little pillow under your feet again. Or we can share the couch, and I'll hold your feet. Lady's choice."

Maisy bit her lip, enamored by his grin. She enjoyed the exchange more than she should and especially liked the feel of his hands on her. "Fine. If you insist," she said. "You made me dinner. The least I can do is let you touch my feet."

His eyes went dark with faux mischief. "I can touch them?"

Maisy snorted. "You are touching them. They're on your lap."

Blaze stretched his fingers in the air above her fuzzy socks, then lowered his hands to her ankles, peeling the polka-dotted fleece away. She shivered as he pressed the pads of his thumbs against her tender arches, working in small, muscle-melting circles.

She groaned unintentionally, and his big hands closed over her feet in response.

"I'm doing okay?" he asked, a note of pride and more than a little smugness in his tone.

"Mmm-hmm." Maisy braced herself against a flash of other times Blaze had been smugly responsive to her little moans.

He watched her as he massaged, his gaze

gliding over her body, lingering on her parted lips before looking into her eyes. "Feeling more relaxed?"

"Very." Her cheeks went hot again, this time with clear and perfect memories of his hands all over her in the very best ways. "Don't stop," she said, allowing her head to drop against the pillow behind her and her eyes to fall shut. She'd said those same words to him more times than she could count. She wasn't sure when a foot rub had ever gotten her so worked up, but she liked it. And she blamed the pregnancy hormones.

"Can I ask you something?" Blaze's voice was low and smooth.

"Anything."

His fingers stilled for a half heartbeat before falling back into rhythm. "Do you have a name picked out?"

Her eyes opened, and she raised her face to look at him. "Natalie, if it's a girl." To honor her sister. "Blaze, if it's a boy." She pressed her lips together as a flicker of shyness cooled her thoroughly. "If that's okay with you."

He nodded. "Yeah."

"Yeah?"

Blaze cleared his throat, head bobbing and smile growing. "I'd like that. A lot, actually."

The familiar tones of a breaking news story drew their attention to the television, where

Sarah's drawing of the man who'd attacked Maisy and killed Clara appeared onscreen.

Maisy used the remote to increase the volume. Sergeant Maxwell had been immeasurably kind to her when he'd arrived in Blaze's office. He'd promised to have the sketch distributed to every major news channel and media outlet possible before dinner. And it looked as if he'd gotten that done. According to Maxwell, the attacker's image was also being run through facial recognition software. A match would provide law enforcement with a name and profile to use in tracking him, including known associates and addresses.

"We're going to find him," Blaze said, sliding his hands over her ankles and tightening his grip once more.

Maisy had changed into her pajamas while Blaze made dinner. Now, his confident fingers were making their way up the soft cotton material, kneading and massaging her tired calves as they went.

"Still okay?" he asked.

She fixed him with a disbelieving stare. "You know I love this. You know I'm a sucker for all forms of massage. So, what exactly are you up to, Blaze Winchester?" Certainly not a trip to the bedroom. Unless he found women the size of tugboats, and roughly shaped like one, sexually arousing.

He grinned. "I'm just trying to be a good host. Make you comfortable. Show you I'm glad you're here." His expression went serious. "Maybe show you how incredibly sorry I am that you were ever in danger on my watch."

That made more sense. This was an apology massage.

"Not your fault," she said for the tenth time since she'd been attacked. "It is your fault I'm alive, however. Because you had the forethought to arm me with a weapon I could easily access and use. It's also your fault I have a full stomach of nutritious food right now. That all my things are under this roof. And I have a safe, warm, dry place to sleep. Those things are 100 percent on you."

Blaze shook his head in disagreement as she spoke. "You're smart," he said, his magic hands determinedly erasing the stress of her day, and possibly the bones in her body. "Not everyone could have acted as quickly. Thought as clearly. Made the move to escape before being taken." He worked the muscles of her calves with impressive care and expertise, fuzzing up her thoughts. "And it was your idea to talk to Sarah today. You're the reason this guy's face is on television. Now he's on the run." Blaze tipped his head toward the newscast without breaking her stare. "You did that."

A zealous onscreen reporter recapped the uglier details of Maisy's last two days.

"Someone will recognize him," Blaze assured. "People will call in and testify to seeing him at the local gas station or serving him at a sandwich shop. Maybe they'll know his cousin's girlfriend, but they will call." Blaze smiled. "And then we've got him. If we're lucky, he'll flip on his employer in exchange for a plea bargain. Then his testimony can be added to our case at Luciano's trial."

Maisy rubbed her stomach where the muscles began to bunch and tighten across her abdomen. "So, I did okay," she said, working her lips into a little smile. "I guess we make a good team."

"The best," he said, voice thick with promise and nostalgia. "The way I recall it, you and I were good in every way."

Maisy bit her bottom lip and shifted as heat rose through her chest and pooled in her core. Her breasts tightened, and she ached for the complete intimate connection they'd shared so many times before.

But that would have to wait until she could see her feet again, if that was what he was thinking about. Everything else in her life had to wait until the day Luciano was behind the bars of a maximum-security prison, cut off from his network. A day when she no longer had to worry a killer lurked nearby, tasked with her murder.

Until then, she needed to get her head on straight. She had to stop getting lost in the past, wishing things were like they were before. Because everything had changed.

BLAZE WATCHED MAISY, loving her shy smile and the sweet blush across her cheeks. He especially enjoyed knowing he'd put that expression on her face and incited the heat. Being there with her, so comfortably, so casually, was all that he'd dreamed of for a very long time.

Now, here they were. Together again. Despite the hurricane trying to tear them apart.

And he was touching her.

And she was enjoying it.

And the connection felt so powerful, he had to force himself not to press his luck and scare her away. If she still cared for him the way he cared for her, one day soon their life together could be like this every night, minus the danger. He and Maisy could be teammates, conquering whatever life threw at them. Because he and Maisy were great together.

He cradled her feet on his lap, working his

fingers over the soles then the tender muscles of her calves, willing to comfort her for as long as she would allow it. He'd truly missed these simple moments with her, and he hoped selfishly she felt the same way. Everything was easy with Maisy, comfortable and familiar, even when they'd been new to one another. The connection between them was like nothing he'd ever felt before.

And now they had a baby on the way.

There was no denying his incredible physical attraction to her. He doubted any amount of time or distance could have changed that. But it was impossible to know if the feelings were one-sided. Or if she could ever want him again the way she once had. After all, he'd gotten her pregnant, then vanished from her life. Logically, he couldn't have done anything differently, because he hadn't known about the baby, but logic didn't always matter where emotions were involved.

He ran his hands over her calves, stopping to grip the sensitive space behind her knee.

Maisy sucked in a breath, and their gazes locked.

The familiar heat in her eyes sent flames licking through him, spreading like wildfire and tightening his jeans.

"Maisy?"

"Uhm." She averted her eyes, red scorch marks slashing both cheeks. "I should get to bed. I've had a long day, and Isaac said I should rest. Is that okay?" She swung her legs away from him.

"Of course," he said, lifting his hands.

She paused after she stood, apparently conflicted. "Maybe I should sleep on the couch this time. You suffered out here last night."

"I'm fine," he said, dropping his hands to his lap. "How about I walk you to your door?"

She rolled her eyes and huffed a laugh as he stood and followed her toward his room.

She stopped after only a few paces and gripped her middle.

"What's wrong?"

She grimaced, bracing a palm against the wall. "False contraction. I'm fine. It'll pass." She smiled, breathing in strange little puffs. "I just wish these practice runs weren't quite so realistic."

Blaze moved in closer, brushing hair away from her face. "Here." He looped an arm around her shoulders and turned her to him.

She went easily, rubbing her middle and letting Blaze keep her upright as she navigated the evident pain. "I was supposed to begin Lamaze classes by now," she said. "Dr. Nazir recommended them last month, but I put off registering. I figured I'd wait and take the classes once I got back home instead."

"Lamaze?" he asked, gears turning in his head. Classes to prepare women for labor and delivery.

She nodded, expression still tight with discomfort. "I have a birth plan," she said. "I want a natural delivery with dim light and soft music. Lamaze will help me manage the pain."

"Do you need a partner for those classes?" he asked, almost certain most women did. Not that Maisy had ever seemed like any other woman to him.

"Yeah," she said, cautiously. "Usually. Why?"

"I'd like to be your partner," he offered.

Her face snapped up, curiosity and surprise on her brow. "Okay."

He smiled.

Maisy stepped away, breathing a little more naturally. "I should lie down now. I'll see you in the morning?"

Blaze stuffed his hands into his pockets, hating the chill left in her absence. "I'll be here if you need anything."

And just like that, he watched her walk away again.

And he hated it even more this time around.

Chapter Nine

Maisy slept poorly, despite her fatigue, stealing short bits of rest between longer bursts of paranoia and anxiety. The last forty-eight hours had overwhelmed her, and the more frequent Braxton-Hicks had her further on edge. Being pregnant for the first time came with its own amount of subtle panic, and without Clara to reassure her, the fear for her baby was mounting. If she went into labor before her life settled, she wouldn't even know how to handle it. Obviously her painstakingly prepared birth plan wasn't going to happen the way she'd hoped. And she hadn't even had her Lamaze classes yet. With a killer stalking her until the trial, she wasn't sure when she'd ever have the chance to do anything normal again before her baby's birth.

She waited impatiently for the sun to rise and trace a path across the windowsill, then she climbed out of bed. She took her time getting ready for the day, unsure if Blaze was awake and not wanting to disturb him if he wasn't. He'd probably stayed up well into the night, keeping watch and waiting for updates from his sergeant.

When she opened the bathroom door, the scent of brewing coffee and something rich and buttery wafted in to greet her on the air. She followed the sounds and scents of breakfast through Blaze's home, trying not to drool. "You made pancakes," she accused a moment before entering the kitchen.

He peeked over one broad shoulder as she approached, then whistled. "You wake up looking like that?"

"In full makeup and wearing the only outfit I don't completely hate?" she asked. "Absolutely. My hair blew itself out."

He grinned. "The curls are back. I approve."

And Maisy approved of his nicely fitting jeans and simple white T-shirt. His hair was rumpled, and his cheeks were stubble-covered. He looked like the definition of sexy and casual.

"Are you getting used to it?" he asked, reminding her they were still talking about her awful hair.

"No. As usual, I jumped the gun and caused myself trouble." Quick reactions were her specialty. They'd saved her life once or twice lately, but for the previous twenty-six years, her act-now, think-later personality had gotten her into more than one bind. Overpaying for things. Overcommitting to social engagements. And that belly button piercing on her twenty-first birthday. "I could probably get on board with the length, but I don't like the color." She rolled her eyes, then moved to his side, pouring a mug of coffee while he flipped another pancake. "It's a little dumb, but I don't look like Natalie anymore." She inhaled the warm, bitter steam. "I kind of liked that I could still see her in the mirror."

He adjusted the flame under his skillet, then offered a warm smile. "I don't think it's dumb. I don't think she would, either." His gaze slid to the cup in her hand. "Is that okay for you?" he asked, a small crease forming between his brows. "For the baby?"

She narrowed her eyes as she blew across the hot surface of her drink. "Yes." She'd stuck to decaf and herbal tea for months, but she hoped a little caffeine would help clear the fog of fatigue from her brain.

He moved the final pancake to a plate piled ten high. "Right," he said sheepishly. "How about I let you take care of Bun while I take care of you?"

"Excuse me?" she asked. "Did you just call my child Bun?"

"Our child," he said, a flash of intense pleasure in his soft blue eyes. "And yeah, like a bun in the oven."

Maisy squinted, lips pursed.

"Not that I'm calling you an oven," he backpedaled. "Hey, look, I made pancakes."

She took a seat at the table, warmed by his insistence at calling the baby theirs. "This all looks and smells amazing," she said. "Sorry if I'm being cranky. None of the bad stuff is your fault, and I'm really glad I'm here. And that you're here. It didn't occur to me until I'd walked all the way to your doorstep that you could have moved. Or acquired a live-in girlfriend while I was gone. I was stuck in the safe house, but your life was marching on."

Blaze watched her cautiously as he ferried the platter of hotcakes to the table, along with butter, syrup and silverware. Plates were already waiting. "I love this place. I can't imagine leaving it. And my life didn't move on the way you're implying."

"No girlfriend?" she asked, knowing it was unlikely he was seeing anyone and the woman hadn't called or stopped by in two days. Though, she could be traveling, or maybe they'd spoken privately while Maisy was showering or in bed. Anything was possible, and it was better to assume he was taken than assume he was single and learn she was wrong. Her traitorous heart had already imagined them raising their child together, watching the baby age as they grew old in one another's lives.

Blaze settled on the seat across from hers and selected a pancake. "I haven't dated." He shifted uncomfortably, casting a quick gaze in her direction. "I'm guessing you didn't sleep well." He pointed his fork at her coffee when she stared blankly back.

He hadn't dated? In all these months? She took a bigger drink of coffee, busying her mouth against the urge to ask why and if, maybe, it was because of her. "Not really," she said instead, answering his question about her sleep. "It's hard to get comfortable these days. Add everything that has been going on to that, and it's practically impossible. I was lucky the night I got here. I slept like a baby. Did you get any rest?"

"Some. I did a little research after you went to bed. I was curious about the contractions you were having."

She paused, watching him more closely as she helped herself to a pancake. "Yeah?"

He inclined his head. "From what I understand, Braxton-Hicks are par for the course, but I also learned that the amount of physical and emotional stress you're under can cause preterm labor. Which is scary, so we should keep a close eye on the contractions in case one of these days they become more than just little practice runs. And definitely ask your doctor about what you're going through when we see her."

Maisy smiled. "I appreciate that you're a problem solver, civil servant and all-around hero, but I think you're overreacting a little."

He smirked. "You think I'm an all-around hero?"

She laughed. "We'll ask Dr. Nazir about the contractions and see what she thinks."

He released a long sigh, as if he might've been holding his breath before. "How do you stay so calm all the time? Do you know how many things can go wrong in a pregnancy?"

"I'm aware." She forked a bite of pancake and dragged it through a puddle of syrup. Between fears for her baby's health and the possibility of a lurking assassin, she'd rather think about the assassin. Avoiding him was at least something she could control. Or try to. "Any word on the runaway shooter? I don't suppose someone saw him pumping gas and called the police? Maybe he's behind bars right now?"

"Afraid not," Blaze said. "But everyone in

the state is probably looking for him. Maxwell texted earlier to say the FBI put a bounty on his head. One hundred grand to anyone with information leading to his arrest," Blaze said. "So, the public is looking for him just as diligently as law enforcement now. He will turn up."

Maisy breathed easier. "Let's hope someone finds him before he finds us."

A sudden thump on the porch sent a bolt of panic through the air, and Maisy's fork clattered to her plate.

Blaze was on his feet before she took her next breath, gun drawn.

Her gaze darted across the front windows, searching for shadows, for signs the killer had found her.

"Stay here," Blaze instructed, and he moved carefully toward the door.

BLAZE BRACED HIMSELF to defend Maisy and their child. The urge to fight tightened his muscles as he moved. The desire to rain a world of hurt down on whoever dared to come for her fueled his steps. He leaned a shoulder against the wall and peered around the edge of his curtains, scanning the empty gravel drive out front. A puff of dust drew his attention to the bicycle making its way back to the road.

"Newspaper," he said, chuckling lightly before opening the door.

Maisy heaved a sigh behind him.

He carried the paper to the table and returned his gun to his holster.

"I don't need any more coffee," she said pressing both palms to her chest. "I think I just had three consecutive heart attacks."

Blaze went back to his pancakes, smiling, but on edge. If he'd somehow missed the paper boy driving up to the porch, how could he keep a trained killer off his property?

"What do you know about the other witness who died?" Maisy asked. "We never talked about that. One was killed the day my safe house was attacked, then another was lost yesterday. Was he in witness protection, too?"

"No." Blaze set his fork aside. "This guy was a middle-aged banker who'd laundered money for Luciano a bunch of times over the years. He also witnessed him murder two businessmen who owed him money. One of them was your friend Aaron."

Maisy's jaw sank open. "He wasn't alone that day?" The day she'd lost her sister.

"Seems not, though it's the first I'm hearing about it. Turns out the marshals have been working on a need-to-know basis with information on this case. And they haven't felt the West Liberty PD needed to know much."

Maisy rubbed her forehead. "I will never understand the weird tension between law enforcement entities. Or why criminals like Luciano kill people who owe them money. He can't get money from a dead person. Why not keep him alive? Murder seems counterintuitive to his cause."

Blaze had no real answer to her first question, but he could take a stab at the second. "Once someone like Luciano decides the guy can't or won't ever pay up, killing him sets a precedent for others in his debt."

"Pay or die," she mused. "I suppose that would be a powerful motivational tool for anyone on the fence about running off with his money."

Blaze nodded. "Pretty much."

"So, the man who died yesterday was one of Luciano's own? How do you think he found out the guy was going to testify?"

"That's the question of the day," Blaze said. "No one was supposed to know. Everyone hates the thought of a dirty lawman, but there's a hole in our fence somewhere. We've got too many infiltrations happening right now for anyone to keep claiming coincidence."

Maisy's shoulders slumped. "So we have to

hope the shooter is captured, then agrees to turn on Luciano."

"His testimony would really help." Blaze tried to imagine a scenario where the shooter could be located, captured, then turned before the trial began next week.

Maisy unrolled the morning paper, then shook it open and blanched. "Well, new plan needed." She pushed her plate aside and smoothed the paper onto the table between them. An article with Sarah's sketch and a photo of the same man centered the page. Underscored by a headline announcing he'd been found. Dead inside his car.

Blaze swore, then hunted down his cell phone. He'd left it on his couch when he went to make breakfast. He'd silenced the device before falling asleep, to avoid waking Maisy. Until he'd walked away and left it on the sofa cushions, he'd still heard it vibrate with every incoming message.

He scrolled the missed notifications. The notification of the shooter's death had come from Maxwell an hour ago.

He dialed his sergeant, and the call went to voice mail.

"This isn't good, right?" Maisy asked.

Blaze lifted troubled eyes to her and shook his head. "No." He dialed Lucas next.

"Because, if this guy is dead, it's because some bigger, badder guy is taking over his work?" Maisy asked, attention back on the paper before her.

Lucas's phone rang through to voice mail.

Blaze redialed. Fairly certain as usual that Maisy's theory was correct. And that wasn't good news. "Pick up," he whispered, willing his brother to answer the damn phone.

"How is Luciano doing this?" Maisy asked, her pale skin going a little green. "He's pulling all these strings from jail? He got a second shooter to shoot his original shooter? Who does that? How big is his network?"

"Winchester," Lucas finally answered on a yawn.

"Have you seen the paper?" Blaze asked rhetorically, skipping over the small talk. He had no doubt that Lucas would've called him if he'd seen the headline.

"I just got home three hours ago. I was called back in after dinner last night. Why?" His voice cleared on the final word, as if his brain was finally waking up. "What happened? Are Maisy and the baby okay?"

"Yeah, but the man who attacked her yesterday is dead. Shot inside his car."

Lucas swore, a little more colorfully than Blaze had.

"I'm putting you on speaker," Blaze said, pressing the option on his phone screen, then setting the device on the table. "Lucas. Maisy."

The pair exchanged tense pleasantries.

Blaze pulled the newspaper across the table and skimmed the rest of the small article. Maisy's questions were valid. How powerful was Luciano? And was Blaze being naive to believe he could protect her at his home? "It might be time to take Maisy off the grid somewhere."

"What?" she asked, eyes wide, as his brother wondered, "Where?"

"I don't know yet, but if her attacker's dead this morning, I've got to consider whoever shot him is looking for her now. Someone has surely shared the fact she was with me at the station yesterday. If not, I'm sure they'll be looking at me anyway. Maisy was in my care while we searched for Luciano last year, until she went into protective custody."

Lucas grunted.

Maisy pressed her lips together, brows furrowed. "I'll do whatever you think is necessary, but I have to see Dr. Nazir for my appointment this week. I can't miss that."

"All right," Lucas said. "Let me get dressed and make some coffee. I'll think of some ideas for relocation and call you back."

Blaze disconnected the call, then reached

for Maisy's hand. "We won't miss the appointment," he vowed. "And I don't want you to worry. The move is strictly precautionary. We'll find a nice place with everything you need to be comfortable. Check in under fake names, then relax until the trial. It'll be an adventure. No one will know where we are, and all we'll have to do is pass another week or so playing cards and watching television."

The tension in her jaw and across her forehead lightened. "When you said off grid, I pictured myself eating cold corn out of a can and peeing in the woods."

Blaze barked a laugh. "I swear I will not let things get that bad. We'll spend the rest of today making plans then slip away after dark. How about that?"

She squeezed his hand. "Okay."

"Until then," he said, working up a brighter voice and smile, "I found something I want to show you." He stood and pulled her up with him, then led her into the living room, where his laptop sat open on the coffee table. "When I was reading up on your contractions last night, I found these videos on YouTube that I think you're going to like."

"What videos?" she asked, caution creeping into her voice. "I don't want to watch another woman deliver a baby. I've seen it, and it's terrifying."

Blaze moved the laptop to the end of the table, then sat on the floor in front of it. "Sit with me?" he asked, patting the floor in front of him, then opening his legs in a V.

She frowned.

"Trust me." He reached for her, and she sighed before following him onto the floor.

"Will you start the video?"

She dragged a fingertip over his laptop's touch pad, then clicked once before settling between his open legs, folding hers before her. "Lamaze," she said softly. "You found me an online Lamaze class?"

"There were a few with good reviews," he said, "but this one had the most views. That has to count for something, right? If you don't like it, we can watch a different one."

Maisy was still as the woman onscreen introduced herself, listing her experience and qualifications, then gushing over the miracle of motherhood, pregnancy and birth.

"Now you won't have to risk going anywhere to take the class," Blaze said softly, trying not to talk over the class leader. "I can be with you. You'll be prepared, and from what I've read, you can use the breathing techniques to help with pain from your Braxton-Hicks."

He pulled her hair over one shoulder, peeking around for a look at her face.

Maisy leaned against him, tilting her head to reveal a teary-eyed gaze. She pulled his arms around her and smoothed his palms over her bump. "Thank you," she whispered.

And Blaze knew whatever happened between them now, there would never be another woman in his life, because his heart forever belonged to her.

Chapter Ten

Maisy completed her first Lamaze class with Blaze as her partner. The moment was satisfying beyond her wildest dreams. Despite all the bad things that had happened, she could never have imagined seventy-two hours ago that she'd be in Blaze's home again, in his arms and completing a Lamaze class that he'd found online for her.

The smile on her face could possibly be permanent.

"That was good," he said. "What did you think?"

Maisy turned to face him where they sat, then rose onto her knees and framed his face in her hands. "This was the most perfect thing you could have done. It was exactly what I needed. And having you by my side was icing on the cake."

His eyes widened briefly before dropping their focus to her lips and going dark with something that looked a lot like hunger. "You're welcome."

She leaned forward, pressing her forehead to his and basking in the perfect moment. For the first time in what felt like forever, she was relaxed, grounded and at peace.

His hands rose to her waist, tugging her down to him, before slipping his fingers into her hair.

She started at the jolt of electricity that pulsed through her. Blaze's nearness had always affected her that way.

He cupped the back of her head, cradling her, and Maisy's inhibitions fell away.

Lost in the spell he'd always had on her, she pressed her lips to his and let everything else go. Warmth spread through her at the scents of his shampoo and cologne. The gentle scrape of his unshaven cheeks against her palms. The strength of his arms. Breadth of his chest.

His lips parted beneath hers, and she easily opened to receive him. Her heart pounded enthusiastically as he deepened the kiss.

When he moaned into her mouth, lavishing her generously with bone-melting caresses of his tongue, she worried there'd soon be little more than a puddle left of her.

Until then, she embraced it. Allowing joy to ping-pong inside her, erasing all the bad memories and replacing them with red-hot need and want and hope. Her head fell back as Blaze moved his mouth over her chin and down her neck, suckling and nipping in sweet, erotic bites.

She smiled at the ceiling, truly happy and completely relaxed for the first time in months. She soaked up the heat of his lips on her throat and his hands on her breasts until a rush of unbidden and unwanted worries returned. Ruining everything.

Her heart sank, then broke with memories of what had brought her back to him. And reminders that they would soon be on the run from her would-be killer. The icy blast cooled her heated core.

"What's wrong?" Blaze panted, sliding his hands over the curves of her hips. Concern and tenderness warred with want in his eyes. "Are you okay?"

She nodded, biting her lip and hating herself for inciting the kiss, only to pull away. "I'm sorry. I can't."

"Can't kiss me?" he asked. "Or something else?" He released her when she pulled back, stroking her arm and reaching for her hand instead. "You were doing one hell of a job." He grinned, attempting to let her off the hook. "But it's okay if you don't want to anymore."

She nodded, unable to form the right words, if there were any, to explain herself. She just couldn't afford to get lost in another whirlwind relationship with Blaze, easy as that would be. She had more than herself to think about this time. There was a baby on the way who would need 100 percent of her. Whatever she and Blaze were doing, it couldn't continue, and losing him had nearly torn her apart the last time.

A peppy rap on Blaze's front door broke the tension, turning them both toward the sound. The shadow poised beyond the front window leaned forward and pressed cupped hands to the glass.

Blaze groaned. "Derek," he muttered, relaxing his posture as he turned back to Maisy, gentle eyes fixed on hers.

She held her breath in anticipation of whatever he might say.

Instead, he pressed a kiss against her forehead, then rose gracefully and offered her his hand, bringing her up with him.

She went to the kitchen table, thankful for the interruption, while Blaze answered the door. Her hands moved instinctively to her neck and collarbone, tracing the paths of his touch. Her fingertips glided over trembling lips, still sensitive from his kiss. She'd blame her hormones for turning a Lamaze class into a reason to make out on the living room floor, but she was certain her heart had as much to do with that as anything. Why did her life and love have to be so complicated?

A sharp wolf whistle drew her eyes to Derek, the oldest of the Winchester brothers, striding confidently in her direction. His arms were already open to embrace her. "Well, look at you."

Derek, Blaze and Lucas were what Maisy's grandmother called Irish triplets. The younger two were conceived within weeks of the previous boy's birth, keeping their poor mother pregnant for nearly three years straight. A predicament Maisy couldn't imagine. And didn't want to. But she could surely sympathize with any woman married to a Winchester. How could she possible keep her hands to herself?

Despite their close ages, Lucas, the youngest, was distinctly more easygoing than the others. Blaze tended to brood. And Derek had never met a woman he couldn't immediately relieve of her clothing.

"Hi, Derek," she said, tugging nervously on her shorter, now brown hair.

"Miss me?" he asked, wrapping her into a careful hug, as if he might somehow hurt her, or catch her pregnancy.

"Every minute," she said. "How'd you know

I was here?" She looked around him as he released her, seeking Blaze's face.

"Blaze called everyone the minute he heard the good news." He grinned, gaze dropping to her middle.

"Everyone?" she asked, fighting a proud smile.

"Everyone listed under *W* for Winchester in his contacts list, I suspect," Derek said with a wink. "Our mama's fit to die if she doesn't get a look at you soon. She's planning a baby shower for immediately outside the courtroom following your testimony, I believe. I'm bringing potato salad."

Blaze laughed, arriving in the kitchen a moment later, arms loaded with what looked like groceries and a box of doughnuts. "I only called my brothers and parents. Mama did the rest. And Derek brought you food because apparently he didn't think I was feeding you."

"Pregnant women have cravings," Derek said.

"You came over to bring me doughnuts?" Maisy asked, enjoying the simple moment of normalcy. She couldn't wait to see Mr. and Mrs. Winchester again. They'd been so kind to her when they'd first met. They hadn't treated her as if she might break, despite the fact she was mired in guilt and grief. They'd called her strong and courageous.

"While I'm here, I thought we could work up a plan to hide you both for another week or so until the trial," Derek said. "I have strong connections to local law enforcement that keep me informed without obligating me to do anything I don't want to."

"They can order you to butt out," Maisy said, grinning.

"They can try."

"Sounds good," Blaze agreed, setting the doughnut box on his table and the sack of groceries beside it.

"Have you thought about reaching out to the judge or prosecuting attorneys?" Derek asked. "Maybe you can get the trial moved up or find a way for Maisy to give her testimony from a secondary location. Livestream it for the jury."

Blaze reached into the grocery bag, brows furrowed. "The trial's been pushed back three times already. There's no way they'll move it up, but we can ask about a live feed testimony."

"Be prepared for some pushback from the lawyers," Derek said. "They'll claim the jury needs her to be physically present, but the judge knows the situation. He'll have to consider her safety in all this and remember she's one of only two witnesses left."

"You're both assuming the judge isn't dirty," Maisy said, a knot of fear growing in her gut. "Someone definitely is."

The brothers traded pointed looks, then Blaze turned back to the groceries.

She watched in unexpected amusement as he lined up Derek's offerings on the table next to the doughnuts. Licorice and lemon candies. Crackers and ginger ale. A tub of rocky road ice cream. "Two jars of pickles?"

Derek shrugged. "One's dill. One's bread and butter."

"Very thoughtful."

"Thanks. So, when are you due?" he asked, apparently unable to stop staring at her middle. "Blaze was quick to deliver the news. Not so much with the details."

"About six weeks," she said. Luck willing.

"Boy or girl?"

"I don't know yet."

He scrunched his smug, handsome face. "Why not?" He hiked his brows when she only shrugged in response, then crossed his arms and leaned against the counter to stare at her.

She laughed. "I'd nearly forgotten how shy and unintrusive you are."

Blaze hauled the pickles to the refrigerator. "We'll know when we know, brother. For now, let's work on that plan for anonymous lodging, then set up arrangements for check-in, wherever we're headed."

Derek grinned wickedly. "All right. One more question."

Maisy crossed her arms and glared back. "If you ask me what I weigh, I will force-feed you all those dills."

"Have you thought of Derek for a boy name?" he asked, a hint of sincerity in his normally cocky tone.

"Hey," Blaze answered, smiling broadly as he slipped into the space at Maisy's side. "Get your own baby. This one is mine."

Maisy laughed. "How about we buy you a World's Best Uncle mug?" she suggested. "We can have Derek put on that."

Derek considered the offer briefly. "Make it a shot glass, and I'm in."

"Done." Blaze poured his brother a cup of coffee and ferried it to the table. "I'm open to suggestions on locations. We can stay under an alias without trouble and pay in cash," he said. "Not too far outside the city limits. She needs to be within fifteen minutes of a hospital. I don't want to take any chances if she gets hurt or sick."

Derek accepted, then sipped the coffee. "You also don't want to be too close to town, or anywhere a series of traffic cams or storefront surveillance videos could give you away."

Maisy listened as the brothers volleyed ideas. They were so much alike, yet so different. It reminded her of her relationship with Natalie. They'd been identical in appearance, but cut from two completely different cloths. Natalie had always been brave and bright, a wild little flame, ready to catch the world on fire. Maisy had been content to observe, never interested in sharing the spotlight. Too afraid of getting burned.

"There are some older motels on the edge of town," Blaze continued. "What do you know about those?"

"Nothing good," Derek admitted. "Prostitutes. Petty crime. Terrible dining options. What about that ritzy spa in the mountains? It's a little farther away, but they've got a doctor on staff."

Maisy's toes curled in hope. She'd never been to an actual overnight spa, but she could get behind spending a week at one.

Blaze lifted his brows, not seeming to hate the idea, either.

The sudden explosion of his front window elicited a scream from Maisy's core. Confusion overtook her as shards of glass cascaded across the wooden floor, skittering in jagged luminescent splinters. Something hard landed in the entryway and rolled in their direction, emitting a thick, acrid smoke.

Both brothers drew their weapons as Maisy fought to make sense of what was happening.

"Get down," Derek called, marching stealthily forward, gun drawn.

Maisy crouched, hands over her head and eyes tearing as the smoke began to fill Blaze's cabin. Nothing made any sense, yet it was all incredibly clear.

Blaze's home was under attack.

"SMOKE BOMB," BLAZE GROWLED, opening one arm wide as he positioned himself in front of Maisy, eyes trained through the growing cloud.

"He's coming in," Derek said, crouched low and gun raised. Acknowledging the obvious.

The only reason to use a device like this was to gain easy access. Soon he, Maisy and his brother would be blind, disoriented and gasping for air. Easy pickings for whoever had thrown the bomb. That person surely had a gas mask and planned to simply walk inside and kill them all.

But this guy had picked the wrong cabin.

The front door burst open a moment later, barely visible now. The sound of splintering wood assured him the barrier had been kicked in.

Derek vanished in the thick gray smoke.

"Derek." Maisy coughed the word.

"He's got this," Blaze said, unable to name a time anyone had gotten the drop on his big brother. "Stay with me. We'll get out of here."

Maisy's small fingers curled into the fabric of Blaze's T-shirt, and she coughed against his back.

"Cover your mouth," he instructed, softly, gut clenching and fear gripping his throat. "Stay low. Back door."

They moved together a few feet before Derek barreled into Blaze, arms pinwheeling, curses flying. Maisy screamed, and the sound ricocheted through Blaze's heart.

Derek righted himself, wiping a sleeve across his face with a sneer before launching back into the fog.

Unseen things broke and shattered around them, stirring up the chaos and shooting terror through Blaze's veins. There was more than one assailant, he realized with a start. The shooter had worked alone, but it took more than one criminal to storm a cabin.

A gunshot rang out, and ice washed through Blaze's veins.

Maisy pressed her face into his back, no doubt recalling the last time she'd been under siege like this and lost a friend.

He reached for her arms, pulling her to his side, then rushing her toward the back door. They needed fresh air and the space to dial 911. If they could circle back to the driveway and get Maisy behind the wheel of his truck, Blaze might even be able to come back and help his brother.

The plan was forming in his head when a second explosion stopped him short. Light flowed through the hazy space where the rear door had once been.

And a form appeared in the haze. A fist connected with Blaze's head before he could turn back. He fell against Maisy, pinning her against the wall.

She screamed, then ducked free, coughing as she vanished into the smoke.

Blaze blinked burning, watering eyes, unsure which direction was up when the second hit arrived, knocking him onto the floor. His training kicked in a heartbeat later, spurred by fear of Maisy's absence, and realization of what that absence could mean. His leg shot out on autopilot as years of hand-to-hand combat training jerked into motion. His foot connected hard with his intruder's torso, eliciting a low, guttural response. Blaze jerked upright on the next breath, fueled by rage and resolve. He landed two sharp punches against his assailant before dropping the man like a sack of potatoes. He didn't get back up.

"Maisy!" Blaze turned in the smoke, eyes stinging and blurred. His throat burned with every breath. His lungs screamed in protest of the polluted air.

Something looped around his throat and tightened, cutting off his limited oxygen. And his world began to shimmer.

Blaze clawed at the rope, cutting into his skin, twisting his body in an attempt to break free.

And a hail of gunshots erupted, illuminating the hazy cabin in muzzle flashes. He threw both elbows backward, aiming and missing his attacker, then the rope tightened again. His knees went weak, and his vision tunneled to a pinhole.

Then Blaze's attacker collapsed behind him, releasing the rope as he fell.

Blaze crumpled forward, gulping poisoned air and coughing against the intake.

Maisy dropped an iron skillet before him, then latched onto Blaze's arms and dragged him toward the broken-in door.

Chapter Eleven

Blaze stood beside the open ambulance doors while Isaac examined Maisy. She'd somehow managed to escape the attack on his cabin without any apparent injuries, despite being unarmed, untrained and seven months pregnant. More than that, she'd saved his life.

Blaze had already called her obstetrician to request her appointment be moved up. The doctor had easily agreed to make room for her first thing tomorrow morning. They'd go to the ER now if Isaac thought it was necessary. Otherwise it was time to pack up and get out of town.

"I'm fine," she complained around an oxygen mask while Isaac continued to monitor her vitals. "The baby's having a party, and I feel better than I have in days."

"It's the adrenaline and oxygen," Isaac told her, working the stethoscope out of his ears and looking strangely at Blaze.

"What?"

His brother frowned. "I'm not sure. Come in here a sec."

Blaze climbed into the ambulance, every fiber of him on full alert. "What's wrong?"

Isaac handed the stethoscope to Blaze. "Put this on. Tell me if you can hear this."

Blaze obeyed without question and looked to Maisy, terror-stricken and praying it didn't show.

Isaac pressed the chest piece against her bump, and it jumped.

Blaze's eyes widened. It was the first time he'd seen Maisy's bare stomach since their reunion. The first he'd ever seen a child moving inside its mother. *His child*, he recalled fiercely, and an instant lump formed in his throat. If something was wrong with their baby…

Isaac moved the chest piece, setting it a few inches away, then looked to Blaze. "How about now? Does that sound right to you?"

Blaze glared back. He had no medical training. If Isaac suspected something was wrong, they should be on the road, doubling the speed limit to get help for his family, not running the hunch past an untrained, inept detective.

"Listen, please," Isaac encouraged.

A small thrumming registered.

Blaze felt his lips part and his chest tighten, as if the tiny sound was connected directly to his heart. "That's—"

"Your baby," Isaac said proudly. "A fine, strong heartbeat, for what I can only assume is a completely healthy child. The obstetrician will likely perform an ultrasound tomorrow and look at each finger and toe, but I don't have any reason to think you need an immediate trip to the ER."

Blaze stared at the place where his child squirmed just below the surface, the steady lub-dub, lub-dub, repeating in his ear. He raised blurring eyes to Maisy.

She caught a tear rolling down her cheek and laughed. Her bright smile was pure pride. True joy. He returned the stethoscope to Isaac without taking his eyes off Maisy, then rested his ear against her middle.

Maisy laced her fingers into his hair and stroked the strands from his forehead as he listened for a heartbeat he could no longer hear and enjoyed the subtle motion of their baby inside her.

"I'll give you three a moment," Isaac said, climbing down from the bay.

Outside, a crowd of law enforcement officials had gathered beside a collection of vehicles. Police cruisers. Government SUVs. A fire truck and other ambulances, along with their drivers and passengers, rounded out the heavily armed circus. Two men were in custody— one shot in the shoulder by Derek, and the other with significant head trauma, thanks to Maisy and Blaze's grandmother's wrought iron skillet. Neither man was carrying any form of identification. And they weren't talking.

"Stop me if I'm ruining the moment," Maisy said softly, "but all those lawmen aren't making me feel any safer."

Slowly, Blaze forced himself upright, unsure what to say. There weren't words. He'd thought the same thing more than once since the caravan of vehicles had begun to arrive. Someone involved in this case was dirty. And it could be any one of the men and women outside right now. "Agreed."

Derek strode across the grassy lawn toward the ambulance, a reluctant smile on his smug face. "How are you guys doing?"

"Good," Maisy answered, tugging her shirt over her exposed stomach. "You?"

"Not a scratch on me." He squared his shoulders. "Unlike the goons in the other ambulances."

"You shot someone," she said, softly. The words were thick with compassion and concern. "That's got to be hard."

Derek frowned dramatically. He bent, then straightened, his pointer finger in the air a few times. "Nah. It's pretty easy. You just—" He turned the finger gun toward a nearby medical kit and gave a few pulls before blowing across the tip. "Anyway. He'll be fine." He pretended to holster his finger. "I never go for the kill shot. I like to see them suffer."

"Lovely." She smirked. "I guess I worried for nothing."

Blaze smiled. No one called Derek on his nonsense faster than Maisy. He could almost see her at their big family dinners, passing an infant to Blaze, taunting Derek and helping his mother harass his father.

"What?" Derek's voice drew Blaze back to the moment. He stared, confused.

"Nothing." Blaze shook off the little fantasy. It was time to get his mind out of the clouds and back on the situation at hand. "Think I can get Maisy out of here without a tail?"

Derek grinned. "Give me a few minutes to talk to the marshals and uniforms." His gaze swept over the cluster of lawmen in the driveway, then narrowed on Blaze's cabin. "Leave your house key, and I'll board up the broken window and deal with the busted doorjambs. Mom will want to handle the mess inside."

Blaze worked the key off his ring and planted it in his brother's hand.

Derek fixed Maisy with a prideful smile. "You did good in there. Protected yourself, my niece or nephew, and my brother. I owe you for that."

"I'm counting on it," she said. "You can start by helping Blaze keep me alive until the trial."

"Already on it," he said, tossing the key into the air, then catching it. He winked before jogging away.

Thirty minutes later, the congestion in the driveway had thinned to Derek and Blaze's trucks, a cruiser and a crime scene SUV. The ambulances had gone, along with most of the lawmen. Derek leaked the story that Blaze and Maisy were headed to a spa outside town until the trial. He'd booked a room for them to help cement the cover, then loaded Blaze's truck with their bags.

A crime scene unit worked methodically through the mess inside Blaze's home, but Derek would stay to see the place secured and cleaned when they finished.

Blaze kept a heavy foot on the gas pedal as they fled town, though he had no plan, and no idea where he was going. A good thing, because if he didn't know the destination, no dirty lawmen could, either.

"We can rent a home from one of those vacation rental websites," Maisy suggested. "Or stay at a bed-and-breakfast under false names."

"False identities are a good idea, and I want to be able to pay in cash. If you feel safe waiting in the car, once we decide where we're going, I can check in alone. Then, anyone stopping by to ask about a couple with a pregnant lady won't find us."

He adjusted his grip on the steering wheel, longing to keep driving until the truck ran out of gas. They could take a cab from there. Stop at the nearest airport, then hop a flight out of the country. Hell, he'd leave the planet if he thought it would keep Maisy and their baby safe. But it wasn't that easy. She needed to see Dr. Nazir in the morning.

A small rusted sign at the next crossroads caught his eye and moved his foot from the gas pedal to the brake. Brandy Falls, just ten miles ahead.

"I have an idea." Blaze hit his turn signal, though there wasn't anyone on the road behind him, and headed up the mountain.

"The ski resort?" she asked. "The season won't open for another month."

"Exactly." Off-season meant an affordable rate, available lodging and no crowds.

Blaze navigated the winding, hilly roads,

following signs toward the lodge. He'd never been much of a skier, but he'd been in the area more than a few times. Hiking in warmer weather. Snow tubing in the winter. "The national park butts up against land owned by the resort. There's a lot of rough terrain this far out but some worthwhile views if you manage the trails. The resort has cabin rentals—there won't be any prying eyes for miles this time of year."

"No well-meaning staff or other guests to spot or recognize me from the news," Maisy said.

He smiled, more confident in his decision by the minute. "We're only about fifteen or twenty minutes from the nearest hospital and your doctor," Blaze said. "A quick drive down the mountain to anything you might need if it isn't available at the general store."

In short, the ski resort was a perfect hideout.

MAISY WATCHED THE beauty passing outside her window. She'd always loved the national park but never knew it stretched this far west. She wasn't a skier, so the entire area was new to her. Unfamiliar, but breathtakingly gorgeous this time of year. Any leaves still clinging to the trees were dressed in an array of color from gold to crimson and eggplant. The road was lined in them.

A small mom-and-pop shop appeared around the next bend, and Blaze hit his turn signal. "General store," he announced, veering into the empty, narrow lot out front. "I'm going to run in and buy a few groceries. Do you need anything?"

Signs in the store's window proclaimed it to be "one-stop shopping." Buy groceries. Order a pizza. Pick up the essentials. Even order flowers.

Her gaze caught on a pink flyer with the image of a bouquet and logo for a national florist. Four words printed beneath had her unfastening her seat belt.

Show someone you care.

"Mind if I come with you?" she asked, already opening her door.

Blaze hesitated before apparently realizing the question was rhetorical and releasing a reluctant sigh.

They made a trip around the store's interior perimeter together before splitting up to shop. Maisy made her way to the counter, hands shaking as memories of the safe house shootout raced in her mind. Clara's funeral had been announced on the radio. A local station was organizing a donation fund for her family. Maisy couldn't attend the service or say a proper goodbye, but she could send flowers. Clara's family should know she cared at least that much. If she survived the trial, Maisy would find a way to apologize in person. To let them know how much Clara's loss hurt her, too. And that she'd died the same way she lived, fighting to protect others.

An older man behind the counter smiled when he saw her. He slid a pair of glasses from the shirt pocket of his blue flannel and placed them on his nose. "How can I help you?" he asked brightly, either a true people person or bored from the lack of human interaction on the mountain this time of year.

"I'd like to order flowers," she said, scanning a colored pamphlet on the countertop.

"We can make anything you'd like if you don't see something you want," he said. "I just punch it into the computer and a florist near the delivery site works it all out."

"It's okay," she said, realizing belatedly that she had to pay cash and didn't have much left. "I'll take this one." She chose an embarrassingly small arrangement, then signed the card with her initials.

"No message?" he asked. "Is this for a friend or family?"

"It's for a funeral," she said, the word lodging painfully in her throat. She completed the order form with details on Clara's upcoming memorial service, then passed the man her money and wiped her eyes. "Thank you."

She took her time searching for Blaze, pulling herself together with each step. She found him crouched before the dairy case.

He squatted next to a full shopping basket with one kind of fruit juice in each hand. The basket brimmed with healthy foods, and he looked at the juice labels as if he might soon get an aneurysm.

"What are you doing?" she asked, sniffing back the leftover emotion that ordering flowers had caused.

He looked up, brows furrowed. "Do you need more vitamin C or D? Or is it folic acid?"

She forced a tight smile, and her bottom lip quivered. "What? No doughnuts and pickles?"

"No." He tucked both bottles into his arms and stood with the basket in hand. "Are you okay?"

"I will be," she said.

And she hoped desperately the words were true.

BLAZE PARKED OUTSIDE the lodge at the top of the mountain, then left his gun with Maisy before hurrying inside to rent a cabin. The middle-aged woman behind the counter barely looked at him, attention fixed to a game on her phone. Still, he made a point of telling her he was a Nevada artist, hoping to find his muse in the Kentucky wilderness.

She grunted, took his cash and wished him well.

Cabin Nineteen was roughly the color of moss, blending easily into the surrounding forest, nearly camouflaged by evergreen trees. The driveway was short and directly accessed by a paved looping road. Several other cabins were visible on the trip from the lodge, though there were no indications they were rented. No vehicles in the drives. No smoke rising from the chimneys.

All very good signs.

Blaze carried the last of the luggage inside, leaving the bags in the entryway. The air was stuffy, tinged with bleach and must. Likely unoccupied for months. The walls were paneled. The floors, cabinets and furniture were pine. The look was rustic but clearly fabricated. The front and back doors were visible from the large square space divided into a living room and kitchen, with a small dinette in between.

Maisy appeared from the hallway, her button nose wrinkled. "One bedroom?"

He laughed. "Sorry. I needed to pay cash

for a week and have money left over for necessities. Also, I had to keep up the appearance of being alone." He was thankful he'd had so much cash on hand. He'd pulled a large amount from savings months ago, planning to buy a fishing boat, only to change his mind. He hadn't gotten around to putting the money back in the bank, and for once, the procrastination had worked in his favor.

She leaned a hip against the couch, a smile playing on her lips. "All you Nevada artists are the same, with your watercolors and your one-track minds."

Blaze headed into the little kitchen, where he'd left the groceries, then began to unpack. "Don't worry. I'm going to sleep on the couch." He repeated the fact internally a few times, making sure it sank in.

"Oh, I wasn't worried," she said. "But you realize this couch is barely five feet long, right?" She aimed a remote at the television. "You're six-one."

His phone rang, and Maisy tensed. "It's Sergeant Maxwell." He accepted the call and raised the phone to his ear. "Winchester."

"Where are you?" Maxwell asked.

"Safe," Blaze said. "What's going on?"

Maisy circled the couch, one hand on her bump, then lowered onto a cushion. The channels changed as she searched, presumably for the local news.

"I spoke with the judge," Maxwell said. "He won't move the trial, and he isn't interested in receiving testimony by video, but he agreed to discuss a livestream with counsel and get back to us."

Blaze leaned against the counter, both relieved and hopeful. "That's more than I expected, so I'll consider it a win. Maybe we'll get lucky and the attorneys will both agree."

"And maybe pigs will fly," Maxwell said, "but we won't know until he asks. On that note, I also need to tell you the prosecutor wants to meet with Miss Daniels. He says it's time to review her testimony. He'll prep her for what to expect from the defense and help her hone her responses. Otherwise the defense is guaranteed to poke holes in whatever she says. She can't afford to let them fluster her, sidetrack her or anything else the jury might see as less than convincing. Plan for a couple sessions this week. An hour or so each time. He doesn't want her to feel rushed or pressured, and I'm sure reliving a story like hers will be slow and difficult."

Blaze tightened his jaw. He didn't like the idea of taking Maisy anywhere other than her doctor's office. And the prosecutor's law firm, located inside the local courthouse, seemed especially risky. Any nut trying to kill her before the trial would expect her to show up there eventually. There had to be a better way. "I'll reach out to him."

"Good."

After a few more assurances that Maisy was safe, Maxwell agreed to trust Blaze, and the men disconnected. Blaze grabbed a bottle of water and carried it to Maisy on the couch.

She accepted the offering easily. "Thanks." After a long sip, she set the drink aside and looked to him with worried eyes. "What did your sergeant say?"

"You have to meet with the prosecutor this week and practice your testimony. He'll review everything he plans to ask you, then prep you for the defense's cross-examination. I'll set the appointment tomorrow. For now, let's just take the rest of the day to settle in and breathe."

She nodded, turning blankly to a rerun on the television. A sitcom from Blaze's childhood.

He looped an arm around her shoulders and tugged her against his side. "You want to talk?"

"No." She rested her head on his shoulder. "Natalie loved this show."

He tipped his cheek against her head and held her.

She watched silently until the next commercial break. "I hate that this is my life right now," she said quietly. "I hate that Nat's gone, and that I have to do this without her. I hate that she went back for Mom's book that day when I should've just let the book go or gone after it myself."

"You didn't ask her to do it," he said. "It wasn't your fault." They'd had this conversation before, but he knew she could never hear his response enough. "Natalie went to get the book because it was important to you, and you were important to her. She wanted to help you."

"She didn't want to die for me," Maisy snapped, voice cracking. "But she did."

"Neither of you could have known. No one could have guessed Aaron was in debt to Luciano. Your instincts told you Aaron was shady. Assuming he was seeing someone else makes a lot more sense than thinking he was about to be murdered by a crime boss."

"She called me to tell me about the car in the drive," Maisy said. "She sent me a picture of it. Then she sent me a video of Luciano with his hands around Aaron's throat. I heard the gunshots. I was on the line while she watched Luciano kill Aaron. I heard her scream, listened as she drove away, terrified, describing it all to me. Luciano said Aaron owed him money and made him look foolish, so he wasn't getting any more chances to do the right thing. That's the price for damaging a psychopath's ego, I guess. The same price Natalie paid for being a witness to murder. Luciano choked him and beat him before ending it with three shots. Then he chased my sister down and ran her off the road and into a tree. The coroner thinks she died on impact, but before he found and took her phone, Luciano shot her three times."

"I am so sorry," Blaze said, pressing a kiss against her head and holding her impossibly tighter as her body shook with sobs.

Her hot tears collected on his shirt where her cheek rested.

Her fingers curled into the fabric of his sleeve and held on tightly as the sitcom droned ahead.

And he stayed with her, unmoving, until her grip loosened. And her thin, thready breaths came slow and deep. Until she finally found rest.

Chapter Twelve

Maisy thought of Clara's funeral all night, wishing she could go and hating more than anything that Clara was gone. Attending the service would've given Maisy closure and the chance to say goodbye, but she couldn't imagine her presence making Clara's family feel any better. Maisy had lived, after all. Why had she and not Clara? She pushed the thought away. It didn't matter. Maisy was back on lockdown. Another lunatic out to kill her. She could only hope that no one else would die because of her.

Dr. Nazir popped swiftly into mind. Maisy selfishly hoped the doctor had heard about Clara on the news, because she wasn't sure she could tell that story again. Attending the appointment without her would already be sad enough.

Maisy wandered through her morning routine, barely tasting the tea, fruit or yogurt before her.

Blaze padded into view as she finished her breakfast. He poured a mug of coffee then took the seat across from her. His hair was damp from the shower, and the scent of his soap and shampoo hung around him like a cloud. "You look miserable," he said. "Are you nervous about leaving the cabin this morning?"

"A little," she said, sure that was at least partially true. She didn't feel like mentioning Clara's funeral was today, or how much she wanted to be there, even if Clara's family might not want to see her. Instead, she motioned to the folded blanket and pillow stacked on the cabin's stumpy, utilitarian couch. The furniture piece was sturdy and fine to look at but uncomfortable to sit on. She couldn't imagine sleeping there had been very restful. Which made it seem all the more ridiculous and impractical that she'd been alone in a queen bed while Blaze had suffered all night in the living room. It wasn't as if he hadn't shared her bed before or wouldn't be able to keep his hands off her.

Though she wasn't sure she could be trusted to return the favor. It didn't even matter she was a little in the dumps this morning. Just seeing him made her want to be held by him.

Protected. Touched. "Did you get any sleep?" she asked, forcing a change in the direction of her thoughts.

"A little." His lips formed a small, inauthentic smile that didn't reach his eyes.

Her curiosity budded. She'd been beating herself up internally, wondering if her desperation to make Luciano pay for what he'd done to her sister had ultimately led to the deaths of several more people, like Clara.

But what had Blaze looking so conflicted?

She held his gaze when it flickered to her for the dozenth time in half as many minutes. "What's on your mind, Detective?"

He cleared his throat. "Should we talk about what happened yesterday?"

Her lungs itched with immediate memories of the smoke bomb. The sounds of splintering wood as the doors to Blaze's home were kicked in. The feel of the frying pan in her grip as it connected with the intruder's head. A criminal who, until now, she'd barely spared another thought. Was that what was on Blaze's mind? Had she killed the guy? Her stomach roiled at the thought. "Did you hear something more about the home invasion?" she asked. "About the men who were injured?"

Blaze puckered his brows. "No. Before that." He averted his eyes while she considered what he might mean. When he drew his attention back to her, he looked ten years younger and a little like a kid who'd just stolen a cookie from the jar.

The proverbial lightbulb flickered on, and she blushed. "The kiss," she said, realizing now he clearly regretted it. She'd replayed it gratuitously through the night. Recalling each moment vividly, turning in his arms and reaching for his handsome face. Now her nervous stomach rocked for a new reason. Blaze thought kissing her had been a mistake. Why else would he want to talk about it?

She dropped her hands to her lap, embarrassed and scrunching the napkin she'd placed there in her fists. She'd been dreaming of a world where she and her baby were safe and Blaze was in their lives. Maybe even in a forever kind of way. The heat of humiliation flamed hot across her cheeks.

"I enjoyed helping you with the Lamaze class," he said carefully. An obvious attempt to avoid hurting her feelings.

Her mind filled in the rest. He'd enjoyed the class but hadn't expected to be physically attacked afterward.

She imagined changing her name and moving to Bogotá. Anywhere far enough to start over. Leave her world of crime bosses, assassins and handsome, brooding detectives behind.

Unfortunately, she wasn't a runner. She was cursed with a concrete stay-and-fight disposition. So, uncomfortable or not, she'd have to get through this conversation, then suck up the bruised heart and ego. There were bigger problems on her horizon. "You enjoyed the Lamaze class," she repeated back to him when he didn't go on. She raised her chin, hoping to look stronger than she felt. "And you hoped we could do another one after the appointment this morning?"

"I'd like that," he said. "If you're feeling up to it." He wrapped his long fingers around the steamy mug, still looking unforgivably guilty. "I know your world is in complete upheaval right now, and I don't want to make it more complicated."

She pursed her lips as her heart fell. The tiny piece of her that had hoped she was wrong fractured.

"I want to help you," he continued. "However I can."

"Good." She smiled. "Because I hear I'll need a lot of help after the baby's born. At least in those first few days while I recover from delivery."

His expression changed suddenly. Flashes

of emotion too brief and fleeting to name swept through his blue-gray eyes then vanished, locked behind the careful cop veneer he'd mastered long before Maisy had met him. "Whatever you need."

She forced herself upright, pushed her chair in and delivered her dirty dishes to the sink. There weren't many things she could control in her life at the moment, but she could still walk out of this awkward, miserable conversation. "Right now, I need a shower. I don't want to be late for Dr. Nazir."

BLAZE KICKED HIMSELF MENTALLY, and repeatedly, as he waited for Maisy to return from the shower. He'd also taken his time getting ready this morning, planning what he wanted to say to her about their kiss. He wanted to know why she'd pulled away from him, and if it was possible that he could find a place in her future. Longer than a few days after her delivery.

Kissing her hadn't been part of the plan when he'd found the Lamaze class online. He'd known the temptation would be there, working so closely with her, preparing for the birth of their child. But he'd firmly resolved to let the moment be about her and their baby. Not his inability to keep his hands off her. Then, the moment she'd set a palm against his cheek, he'd fallen straight into the tender, yearning look in her eyes. He went for it, trying to tell her exactly how he felt with a kiss.

He'd been lost for her the moment their eyes had met last year. Something about her energy and presence had spoken to him. No, it called to him. Their relationship had been deeply intimate and wholly unprofessional from the start. It was consuming. Breathtaking. And everything he could have asked for. He'd often wondered what she thought of him while she was away. The detective who'd taken a grieving woman to bed while hunting for her sister's killer. He had to admit, it didn't look good. Now she was back and carrying his child. This seemed like fate. The perfect opportunity to show her the man he really was, integrity and all. But thirty minutes of holding her and watching her smile through a basic Lamaze class had brought him right back where they'd started.

Even finding the video online had been laced with ulterior motive. He'd wanted to impress her. To prove he'd been thinking of her and that he'd heard her when she said she still needed the classes. He'd wanted to give her something good and peaceful in a time filled with tragedy and noise.

He hadn't meant to make it into anything else.

He was supposed to show her he cared about her deeply and beyond their profound physical connection.

When the whir of the blow-dryer silenced, Blaze considered marching down the short hall and knocking on her door. He wanted to tell her he'd botched their earlier conversation and that he hadn't regretted the kiss, if that was what she'd thought. He'd regretted the timing. He wanted her to know he was a safe place for her. And she could trust him to be whatever she needed, without him making it physical. He wanted to remove her problems, not add himself to the list.

He scraped his palm against his cheek, determined to give her room. He'd double down on the task at hand. Keep her safe until the trial. Then she'd take the stand, give the testimony and begin to rebuild her life. If he played his cards right, she might even let him be part of that.

Maisy reappeared ten minutes before they needed to leave for her doctor's appointment, dressed in black stretchy pants and a soft green sweater. Her sharp hazel eyes looked at everything except him. "We should go," she said. "Better to be early than late."

Blaze grabbed his keys, determined to show

her how much she meant, even if he couldn't seem to find the words.

The short drive into town felt like hours as he searched for things to say.

"It's really getting cold this week," he tried. "The weatherman is predicting snow. Should make for some beautiful views from the cabin."

Maisy trailed her fingertips across the window at her side. "Hopefully the resort maintains the roads off-season. I'm nervous enough about talking to the prosecutor without worrying we'll slide off a mountain trying to get to him."

Blaze smiled, thankful the ice between them was beginning to thaw as Dr. Nazir's office came into view. "I'll get you to the appointments and anywhere else you need to go. Whatever the weather," he promised. "I'll rent a snowmobile if I have to."

She laughed, and his heart warmed.

Blaze parked in the small office lot and smiled through the window. "So, which came first, the obstetrician's office or the bakery right across the street?"

Maisy smiled. "I'm not sure, but the bakery gets my business after every appointment. Today I'm thinking about a loaded hot chocolate and a strawberry-filled croissant."

"Done," he assured her, climbing out of the

truck and circling around to meet her. "I don't suppose they serve cheesecake there."

Her eyebrows rose and her head began to nod. "About fifty kinds, and they're all delicious. Trust me. I'm a shameless sampler."

The rapid thunder of an air hammer drew Blaze's attention to a new building going up beside the bakery. Construction workers lined steel girders and peppered the ground level, running every manner of power tool and making an earsplitting racket. A sign near the road announced Coming Soon! Mother Hubbard's Book Cupboard.

"I can't wait for the bookstore to open," Maisy said. "I want to check it out, and I'm tired of hearing all the racket when I come here."

Blaze followed her into the doctor's office, silently planning a day trip to the finished store. They could choose books for their baby's library and top the day off with desserts from the bakery next door. The construction noises lowered to a dull drone as they approached the reception desk. The eyes of every woman in the waiting room followed them.

"Hello." The woman behind the counter beamed at Maisy, then Blaze, and back. "Dr. Nazir asked me to take you right in when you arrived."

Maisy was weighed, then given a plastic cup with a smile.

Blaze waited under the watchful eyes of nurses and other waiting patients.

When she returned from the restroom, they were taken to an exam room, and Maisy climbed onto the table. Framed images of women at every age lined the muted pink walls. Girls flying kites. Grandmothers on porches. Teens lying on their backs in a field.

"I guess they don't see a lot of men around here," he said after the nurse closed the door. "I feel like I've intruded on the girls' club."

Maisy rolled her eyes and pointed to the wall behind him. "All those women were staring at you because you look like that. Don't pretend you don't know."

He turned to face the wall and started at the sight of himself in a mirror. A slow grin spread across his face.

"Stop," she warned, watching his expression in the reflection.

"You still think I'm handsome," he accused.

Something shuffled outside the room, and Blaze's hand went to his sidearm.

"Do not shoot my doctor," Maisy instructed.

An attractive thirtysomething woman froze in the doorway, eyes wide. The words *Alaya Nazir, MD*, were embroidered in blue on her white lab coat. Her wide whiskey-colored eyes darted from Blaze to Maisy, who nearly threw herself off the table at the woman.

"Maisy." She breathed the word, kicking the door shut behind her as they embraced. "Oh, it's so good to see you. I heard about what happened, and I've been horrified by all of it." She released Maisy, then extended a hand to Blaze. "Thank you so much for bringing her."

"Wouldn't have missed it," he said.

"Sit. Sit." The doctor motioned him to a small plastic chair and Maisy onto the table. She grinned at Maisy. "Now, tell me everything. Start with why your friend wants to shoot me."

Maisy laughed, then made a formal introduction.

Dr. Nazir gave Blaze a long once-over. "So this is *the* Blaze Winchester." A little smile played on her lips. "I see." She wagged perfectly sculpted brows.

A deep blush rose on Maisy's cheeks, and Blaze smiled. "Yep."

Dr. Nazir flashed a mischievous look at Blaze, then turned her full attention to Maisy. "You weren't kidding."

The women laughed, and before long, Maisy was lying back on the little paper-covered table. The doctor pressed a device to her bump, and the baby's heartbeat rang out, strong and true. "That's fast," Maisy said. "Faster than I remember. Is that okay?"

Dr. Nazir smiled warmly. "Yes. Quite. Would you like to know your baby's gender, now that you're both here?"

Blaze looked to Maisy, a thrill rocketing up his spine. She didn't look as sure. "Only if you want to," he said. "You've waited this long. I can wait a few more weeks."

She bit her lip, then looked at her doctor.

"How about this," Dr. Nazir suggested. "I'm going to perform an ultrasound and make sure everything looks good. Can't be too careful after the week you've had, and especially after yesterday. If you decide you want to know the gender while I'm working on that, I can show you. If you decide you want to know later, you can call the office."

Maisy nodded. "Okay."

The ultrasound made Maisy cry, and Blaze wasn't too far from it. Seeing the strange black-and-white image of a baby kicking inside her had been more intense than he'd anticipated. If she allowed him to be present at the birth, he wasn't sure he could stay composed.

When the appointment ended, Dr. Nazir delivered strict instructions to Blaze. "Make sure she rests. The amount of physical and emotional stress she's under is no good for any-one, especially not a woman at this point in her pregnancy. She needs to be still. Feet up. Healthy foods. Plenty of water. And peaceful-ness. We want to maintain this pregnancy as long as possible. Understand?"

"Yes, ma'am," he answered, remembering all the scary articles he'd read about premature births. "I'll do everything I can."

"Good." The doctor smiled. "I want to see you again in two weeks."

Maisy made the return appointment at the front desk, then took Blaze's hand as they left the building. "Thanks for coming with me."

Construction noise roared to life as they stepped into the parking lot. Blaze had com-pletely blocked the sounds out by the time they'd made it to the exam room. Now, the jackhammer seemed offensively loud. "I wouldn't have missed it. Will we get to see the baby at the next appointment?"

"Maybe," Maisy answered, pressing her free hand to her ear. "Dr. Nazir has been incred-ibly generous with the number of ultrasounds she's allowed. From what I've read online, most women only get one or two."

Blaze squeezed her hand, his heart full to the brim. "Still in the mood for that loaded hot chocolate?"

"I'm always in the mood for cocoa."

Their strides fell into an easy unison as they reached the crosswalk. *This is how life should have always been*, Blaze thought, folding his fingers with hers.

He almost didn't hear the suddenly revving engine or squealing tires as a black sports car fishtailed out from the alley between buildings and flung itself screaming in their direction.

Chapter Thirteen

Maisy caught sight of the out-of-control car as Blaze jerked her forward. The roar of the engine became the only sound in her world. She wrapped her free arm around her middle as she ran, towed by Blaze toward the sidewalk ahead. Her strides were awkward, her balance hindered thanks to her completely wrecked center of balance. And she knew with a lung-crushing punch that she couldn't clear the car's path in time. A growl of agony ripped from her core. After all she'd been through, a car would be the thing to finish her.

Then Blaze was at her side. No longer dragging her forward. And her feet were off the ground. Swept from beneath her as he pulled her completely into his arms like a child. One swift and fluid motion later, they were nearly airborne as his long legs finished the trip. Blaze launched them to safety, darting between parked cars at the roadside in a wild, adrenaline-fueled leap.

Blaze wrecked his hip on the larger car's grille, setting off the alarm before they landed in a heap on the strip of grass between the curb and sidewalk. He took the brunt of the fall, doing all he could to put himself beneath her. Wind from the racing car whipped over them as it passed, tossing Maisy's hair and blasting road dirt into her eyes. A split second later, her head cracked against the soggy ground and her vision blurred.

"Is she all right?" a woman yelled, rushing from the bakery to their side.

"Yes," Maisy said weakly. Her voice was thin and warbly to her ears. "I don't know," she amended, a rush of emotion flattening her heart. "The baby." An inexplicable numbness settled over her—shock, she supposed. Confusion. And fear. She'd survived the attacking car, thanks to Blaze, but what about her baby?

Blaze rose to his knees. "Call 911," he said. "Tell them there was an attempted hit-and-run, late-model black sports car. Give them the location." He cupped Maisy's face in his hands, expression conflicted. "I'm going to move you." He scooped her up once more with a curse and jogged back across the street with a limp. "Did you hit your head?" he asked, grimacing with every pace. "Can you move all your limbs? Do you have any specific pains?"

Maisy couldn't answer. She couldn't breathe. If Luciano's henchman had hurt her unborn child, or worse, how could she survive it? He'd already taken Natalie and Clara. Her mind shoved the possibility away.

"We need help," Blaze demanded, shoving the door to her doctor's office open with his shoulder. "She's hurt. She took a hard fall. Hit her head, I think. We need Dr. Nazir. Now!"

Patients gasped. The office staff kicked into gear, rushing to aid them.

Maisy's ears rang, and her world tilted as people fluttered into action around her, hurrying out of their way, opening the door to the hall with exam rooms and asking questions as Blaze barreled forward.

A woman in scrubs led them to an exam room. "Put her on the table."

Blaze obliged, a tortured expression on his handsome face.

"Maisy?" Dr. Nazir arrived on the click-clack of heels, concern drawing lines across her tawny brow. "What happened?"

Blaze recapped as the doctor shined a light into Maisy's eyes and a nurse pulled Maisy's shirt up, then loaded her skin with icy goo.

Blaze moved away, giving the medical professionals room. He gripped the back of his neck with both hands, looking more grief-stricken than anyone she'd ever seen. His shirt and jacket were torn and dirty. A collection of bloody scrapes tore across his cheek and forehead.

"Our baby," she choked, afraid he somehow knew something she didn't.

"I'm looking at your baby now," Dr. Nazir said calmly. She drove the ultrasound wand over Maisy's bump. And there was silence.

"Where's the heartbeat?" Maisy cried.

A nurse slipped a pulse oximeter over the tip of Maisy's finger. "Shh," she soothed. "She's okay. Just busy, dodging the transducer." She pointed to the screen as a small white leg kicked out.

Then, the heartbeat began.

"There we go," Dr. Nazir said. "Your little one is all amped up from the action."

A deep relief rushed from Maisy's chest, and a fresh round of tears began. "Sorry," she sobbed.

The nurse handed her a wad of tissues, smiling sweetly. "See? Everything is going to be okay."

Maisy wiped her eyes. She replayed the previous moments, then looked to Blaze, who'd collapsed into the chair against the wall. "Did you say she?" she asked the nurse. "She's okay?"

The nurse looked to Dr. Nazir, then back to Maisy. "You and your baby," she said.

Maisy let a new possibility form. She took a long, deep breath, then a personal inventory. Intuition tugged, and Maisy gasped. "I'm having a girl."

Blaze peeled himself away from the wall, arms collapsing at his sides. He drifted forward, eyes wide and fixed on Dr. Nazir. "Is that true?"

The doctor looked to Maisy. "Do you want to know?"

"Yes," Maisy said, gaze flicking to Blaze for confirmation.

He dipped his chin.

"Then, yes," Dr. Nazir confirmed. "Congratulations, Mom and Dad. It's a girl."

Blaze nearly bowled the nurse over getting his arms around Maisy. He kissed her lips, nose and forehead. Then cupped her face and stared into her eyes. "We're having a girl." The wonder in his voice, sent shivers over Maisy as a single tear rolled over his scruffy, battered cheeks.

"Okay," Dr. Nazir said. "Let's finish this ultrasound. Strong heartbeats are good, but a thorough exam is better."

Blaze's phone rang, pulling him back. He squeezed Maisy's hand before moving to the edge of the room, unwilling to leave her. His switch from supporting dad to hard-nosed homicide detective was instant and seamless. He recapped the events and the car's description in clipped, authoritative syllables while the doctor and nurse tended to Maisy.

When Dr. Nazir finished, she helped Maisy rise from the table.

"Doctor?" the nurse asked, voice tight and drawing the room's attention.

Blaze lowered the phone and moved in Maisy's direction as she turned in search of an answer. "What is it?"

A small circle of blood stained the crinkled paper where Maisy had been seated.

"What does that mean?" Blaze demanded, shoving the phone into his pocket. "What's wrong?"

"It means we're going to get Maisy back onto the table and have another look," Dr. Nazir explained. "A physical exam this time. You're welcome to stay or leave the room. Whatever the two of you decide, but let's move quickly."

Blaze's phone rang.

Maisy's skin went cold. "Go," she told him. "It's okay to leave. Help the police find whoever did this. Dr. Nazir will take care of me."

"Do you want me here?" Blaze asked, eyes hot and fervent. "Say the word."

"You're going to need to undress and don the gown," Dr. Nazir urged.

Maisy stared, unsure, shocked and terrified. What if the ultrasound had been wrong? What if she lost her baby? *Her daughter.* The air squeezed from her lungs.

"Derek," Blaze growled, phone pressed to his ear once more. "Grab Lucas and get up here. Dr. Nazir's office in Fairmont." He recapped the situation as the nurse helped Maisy out of her pants. Her trembling legs were unwilling to hold her.

"It's okay," Maisy repeated. "You can go. You don't have to stay."

The doctor eased Maisy back and pulled the metal stirrups up to hold Maisy's feet.

Blaze's hand curled over hers a moment later, cell phone tucked away. "I'm not going anywhere until you order me away. Even then, you won't get me farther than the outside of this door."

"Thank you," she whispered.

His jaw locked and determination settled in his cool blue-gray eyes as the doctor began her exam.

Twenty long minutes later, Dr. Nazir gave a reluctant nod. "You're both okay. Everything is as it should be. There's no doubt you have a guardian angel, or nine lives. And you're two centimeters dilated," she said. "Try to stay off your feet and rest." She scooted away from the table and fixed her eyes on Blaze. "I realize you couldn't predict or control what happened out there, but I need you take her someplace safe now. I don't care if it's a pyramid in Egypt, but keep her out of danger for at least the next four to five weeks. She can't continue going on like this without consequences. She's long past lucky. Get her off her feet. Help her relax." She swung her eyes back to Maisy. "Don't do anything more than you have to. Don't lift anything. Don't go for long walks. Feet up. No exceptions. And no more stress." She pressed her lips together and tossed her gloves in the bin with an expression of anguish. "Come back to me next week," she told Maisy. "I want to see you sooner so we can follow up. Go directly to the ER if you have any extreme pain, headaches, blurred vision or dizziness. Call me if the bleeding doesn't stop, or gets heavier, by bedtime." She flipped a business card facedown and scratched a number on it. "That's my personal cell phone. Call it if you need anything. Don't hesitate. Either of you." She looked to Blaze. "It's okay if you bring her rolled in bubble wrap. Do whatever is necessary."

Blaze frowned. "Yes, ma'am."

Maisy redressed, then returned to Blaze's waiting arms and prayed they wouldn't need to use that number.

BLAZE SPENT THE afternoon on the phone while Maisy took a long, hot shower and an even longer nap. He checked on her frequently, between calls to his sergeant and brothers, eager to see her smile once more. She was having his daughter! His heart leaped with fear and excitement and a host of countless other emotions every time the thought came to mind.

He loaded wood into the fireplace as the sun began to set, then stoked it with care. The latest weather report had confirmed the earlier prediction of plummeting temperatures and incoming flurries. Possibly even a snowstorm by the week's end. Their cabin would likely see the brunt of whatever was coming, thanks to its position atop the mountain. Thankfully, the little rental had everything they needed, at least for several more days.

With nothing left to do but stir, he put a frozen pizza in the oven for dinner, then crept back down the hall toward the bedroom.

Maisy's eyes snapped up to meet his as he

peeked through the open door. She'd illuminated the bedside lamp and propped herself up with the pillows since his last visit. "Sorry I slept all day," she said. "I didn't realize how tired I was." The glass of water he'd left on the nightstand was empty.

"How are you feeling?" he asked, taking a seat on the edge of the bed.

"Not great," she admitted. "There's a knot on my head, and I feel like the car might've actually run me over."

Blaze frowned as he reached for her, carefully testing the lump on the back of her head. "Is that why you stayed on your side?"

Maisy laughed. "I sleep on my side because lying flat on my back would probably kill me." She waved her hands around her bump in explanation. "Not to mention I'd never be able to get up."

Blaze smiled. "Are you getting hungry? I put a frozen pizza in the oven."

"That sounds great," she said. "Thank you." She looked him over carefully then, scrutinizing. "What did you learn about the case while I was sleeping? Any word on the car or driver who tried to kill us?"

He did his best not to grimace. Today's attempt on her life had gone largely unnoticed by the community. To his significant dismay, only the waitress who initially came to their aid even saw the car. She couldn't describe it beyond the color, and if Blaze hadn't clipped his hip against a parked vehicle, setting off the alarm, she wouldn't have seen that. "Everyone's working on it," he said instead, hoping to sound positive. "Derek's canvassing area homes and businesses, asking about the car and searching for witnesses. The construction noise masked the engine's sound and your scream, so we haven't had as much response as we'd like."

"No one heard a thing," she said, tone solemn.

She was right. Most folks had no idea anything happened until the police arrived.

"Is Derek having any luck?"

"So far, the people he's spoken with haven't recognized the car's description, but that's not a bad thing," he assured. "It might be a lead. We're thinking the owner isn't from Fairmont. A car like that would stick out in a small town. Someone would have known who it belonged to, or at least remembered seeing it around." It was a long shot to think the new hit man was from the area, but on the off chance the ride was stolen, which could've provided another clue to his identity, it was worth taking the time to ask.

Maisy wound and unwound a loose thread from the comforter around her finger. "No witnesses. That seems about right, given my recent record of awful luck."

"This isn't over yet," Blaze assured. "Lucas is requesting surveillance footage from every business on the street with a camera." Though he hadn't had much luck the last time Blaze spoke to him. Most of the cameras were useless. Dummies meant to dissuade criminals. Or broken and collecting dust. The few feeds of footage Lucas reviewed hadn't provided a clear view of the license plate or driver, but Blaze kept that to himself. Lucas wasn't finished yet.

"And the marshals?" she asked, skin going pale, as it always did at the mention of that branch of law enforcement.

"They're pressing Sergeant Maxwell to have you returned to their protection."

Her jaw sank open. "Are they insane?"

Blaze set a hand over hers, stroking her soft skin and stilling the busy thread on her finger. "Maxwell won't order me to return you. And if he did, you know I wouldn't listen. We've just got to stay here and keep a low profile a few more days. Then the trial will be over, your testimony given, and the worst will be behind us."

She wiggled free from his grip, abandoning the thread and folding her hands with a frown.

"It's not so bad, is it?" he asked, hoping that being stuck alone with him wasn't somehow a worse predicament to her than being hunted by hit men.

"I don't particularly enjoy feeling useless," she said. "But I'm not sure what I can do about it."

Blaze crawled over Maisy's legs and sat beside her at the headboard, crossing his ankles and trying to look at ease. "You're not useless. You're on a very important mission, and your job is to keep your feet up. So far, you're doing great." He nudged her playfully. "Bonus points because I know how much you hate being idle."

"So do you." She sighed. "Now you're stuck on the sidelines, too, because of me."

He turned his head to face her, waiting for her to look his way. "Hey."

Her mouth pulled down at the corners as she brought her warm hazel eyes to his.

"There is nowhere else I'd rather be." He scooped her hand in his, then raised it to his mouth for a gentle kiss. "I say we take advantage of this little time-out we've been given. It's the perfect opportunity for us to catch up. A lot's happened in the last six months, and

I want to hear all your stories. We can sleep late and nap in the middle of the day. You can soak in a tub until the water goes cold and your skin turns pruney. How often do adults get to do any of that?"

She smiled. "I suppose it won't be long before I'm wishing I had time to sleep at all."

"Exactly. And you know what we can do right here, for hours, without even leaving this bed?"

Her cheeks darkened and a smile formed. "What?"

Blaze slipped a hand into the pocket of his hooded sweatshirt and produced a deck of cards. "You still like to play poker?"

Maisy barked a laugh, eyes twinkling. "You still like to lose?"

"I never liked to lose," he said, shaking the deck from the box. "I just didn't mind how happy it made you to beat me."

Blaze shuffled, and Maisy dealt.

They played cards and talked until the oven dinged. Then they ate in bed, picnic-style. Poker, pizza and microwave popcorn. Maisy's laughter erased the misery of the day and filled his head with images of a possible future. Long, lazy days with his best friend. He shook the image away, determined not to get ahead of himself. He'd already kissed her once, and she'd been very clear when she said she couldn't.

Blaze was deep into his losing streak when it occurred to him how wrong he'd been about his relationship with Maisy. He'd thought of his behavior in their early days as unprofessional and inappropriate, because he'd focused on the marathon sex and their powerful physical connection. But he and Maisy were much more than that. They'd done everything together in the short time they'd shared. From cooking and shopping to bonfires and laundry. And it had started with an easy and natural friendship that bloomed into something fast and fevered. But the fever didn't lessen their bond—it had strengthened it.

"Do I have sauce on my face?" she asked, grinning mischievously. "Why are you smiling at me like that?"

Blaze shook his head, awed and pleased by his epiphany. "I really missed you," he said. "I missed this. Us."

She bit her lip, and a sweet pink blush rose across her fair skin, backlighting her freckles. "Me, too."

"I don't regret kissing you," he said, surprising them both with the unplanned confession.

"You don't?"

"No." His voice was low and rougher than

he'd intended, but he pressed ahead. "You already have enough pressure. I didn't want to add to your problems, or be that guy."

"Who?"

"The handsy detective who is supposed to be protecting you but won't keep his lips to himself." He grinned.

"I like your lips," she said, gaze flicking to his mouth. "And your hands. Besides, I'm the one who kissed you. Not the other way around."

Blaze replayed their kiss for the hundredth time. Maisy might've been the one to lean in, but he'd been the one aching to get his hands on her since the moment she'd arrived. And she'd been the one to stop it. "You also ended it."

"Because I felt guilty," she said. "There I was, enjoying myself when other people were being killed because of me."

"You're allowed to be happy, Maze," he said. "People are being killed because Sam Luciano is a psychopath, and that has nothing to do with you. Your lost loved ones would want you to have these moments. To live loudly and profoundly and fill every second with joy. I'd offer to take you anywhere you want to go and do anything you want to do, if we weren't under orders to stay right here and relax."

The blush returned to her cheeks as she looked up at him from beneath her long dark lashes. "Since we're here. Would you be interested in helping me relax?"

The moan that poured out of him wasn't intentional, but it was fitting. "Are you sure about that?"

Maisy nodded shyly, and Blaze climbed off the bed. He gathered the remnants of their picnic and card game, piling it all on a chair in the corner. He returned with a broad, Cheshire-cat smile. "Have anything specific in mind?"

Maisy's hands went to the collar on her nightshirt. She dragged a single pink fingernail along the place where the soft fabric met. "I hear skin-to-skin contact is incredibly comforting."

A breath of air escaped him in a hiss as she freed the first tiny button.

He watched intently as she continued the chore. When the material parted, exposing a silky bra and full, beautiful breasts, he climbed back onto the bed, drawn like a bear to honey.

Her thin fingers tugged the hem of his hoodie upward, and Blaze peeled the layers off his torso. He tossed the shirt and hoodie onto the floor, then waited for her next command.

"A massage would be very relaxing," she said. "We could start with that." Her narrow brows rose in question. "I'm not really supposed to exert myself, but kissing also sounds quite nice."

Blaze's rigid body went impossibly tighter with anticipation of all the things he wanted to do to her. Each of which were guaranteed to leave her boneless. And he wouldn't have to remove another stitch of his clothing.

Chapter Fourteen

Maisy soaked in a warm bath before breakfast, her limbs loose and mind in a haze. She hadn't had any additional bleeding after they'd left the doctor, and she'd held Dr. Nazir's assessment close to her heart. She and her baby were okay. The relief and comfort in that knowledge had made her brave. She'd asked Blaze for exactly what she'd wanted, and he'd delivered.

Flashes of the things Blaze had done to her were enough to steam the mirror. His mouth was magic, and he'd used it on every inch of her. Slowly and gratuitously. It was the first time she'd been touched in months, barring their kiss on his cabin floor, and it had felt exactly right, the way it always had with Blaze. She closed her eyes briefly, savoring the memories.

Blaze had been right about them. He and Maisy shared a bond that was bigger than she'd given credit. They'd been instant friends, confidants and allies from the start. The chemistry and physical attraction were the icing, not the cake. All those factors together made them stronger, not weaker, and no outside force would pull them apart.

She smiled as she toweled off and dressed, choosing a soft cream-colored V-neck sweater and a fresh pair of comfy cotton leggings. The cabin was warm and cozy. Rich scents of freshly brewed coffee and warm buttered toast met her in the hallway, accented by the soft crackle of a fire. Under other circumstances, time alone with Blaze in this cabin would be the stuff fantasies were made of, but the nightmare of their reality kept scratching its way in.

Blaze spotted her immediately, rising from his place at the small dinette, where his laptop sat open. His warm gray eyes and sweet crooked smile belied the fierce protector she also knew him to be. The fact he saved this side of himself for her alone made her dizzy with appreciation and gratitude. He moved toward her on bare feet, then pressed a tender kiss to her forehead. "How are you feeling?"

"Rested," she said. "Peaceful, and trying not to wait for the next shoe to drop."

He pulled out a chair at the table for her. "There hasn't been much news through the night on your case. Who knows? Maybe we'll have a shoe-free day."

"That would be a first," Maisy said. "But a girl can hope."

Blaze made a trip to the counter and returned with a cup of herbal tea and plate with toast and fruit. "Hungry?"

"Yes, and this is perfect," she said. "I promise to make it up to you after we get out of here."

He laughed. "You're doing far more for me right now than I can ever do for you," he assured, smiling at her bump. "So we probably shouldn't keep score."

"You wouldn't say that if you weren't so accustomed to losing to me." Maisy grinned as she raised the mug to her lips. She'd been struggling for months with her complicated life and emotions, but seated there with Blaze looking at her like he was, she knew one thing for absolute certain.

She was deeply, unequivocally in love with him.

Blaze fielded phone calls and worked on his laptop after breakfast while Maisy watched the first snowflakes fall. She read to her bump before lunch, then napped and laughed with Blaze afterward. She had nowhere to go and no one to answer to. And he was right—she loved it.

She curled on the couch in time for the evening news. Blaze arrived with two glasses of ice water and a kiss. He set the drinks on the coffee table, then slid an arm around her shoulders. "You look good."

"I feel good," she answered truthfully. "How's your work going?"

"Derek's at the station, pretending to visit Lucas, but doing his best to pick up on new information. He says the marshals who arrived after my cabin was invaded are meeting with Maxwell. Two suits from the FBI were on their way out as he arrived. No word on what that was about, specifically. I haven't had a chance to speak with the sergeant. Lucas's staying in touch, but there was a rape on campus that's kept him away most of the day, working with the college's security team."

"Do you think the marshals are trying to regain control of my security?" she asked, a shiver rocking down her spine.

Blaze's jaw tightened, and he grimaced. "Yeah, but I'm confident Maxwell will avoid giving me the order to turn you over until his job is threatened. If the marshals get the mayor's ear, and he demands it, Maxwell will have to follow through. Hopefully it won't come to that. He knows I won't comply."

Worry twisted Maisy on the cushion. It was nice that Blaze and his sergeant were willing to do what they could to protect her, but completely unfair that they could be punished for it. "Will you lose your job?" Her stomach ached at the thought. Blaze loved being a detective, and he was incredibly good at it. "If Luciano can puppeteer all these people to come for me, and intercept a marshal who was sent to transport me, it seems reasonable that he could get the mayor to fold for him, as well."

Blaze shrugged. "Maybe. It won't matter. Protecting you is the right thing to do, regardless of any orders that come down."

"It's not fair." She sighed as the words registered to her ears. "None of this is, I know, but I hate how wide the path of destruction is becoming."

"Don't worry about that," Blaze said. "Maxwell will only give the order if he has to. And I'll understand if he does. He shouldn't lose the thirty years he's worked toward retirement or put a big black mark on his otherwise stellar career over this. Not when he can give the order and know I will ignore it. I'd rather lose my job than put you in danger. I can get another job. I can't get another you."

She leaned her head against his shoulder, sad and helpless. At least the trial was only six days away. "Any idea who's working with Luciano from the inside?"

"Not yet." His head tipped against hers, and he stroked her fingers with his own.

The news covered a local flower show and other community and celebrity puff pieces before turning to the Luciano case. A photo Maisy recognized from a few days before appeared in the bottom corner of the screen. The caption: Gene Franco, Missing US Marshal, Found Dead.

Maisy's stomach rocked as a reporter covered the story from the scene. A flurry of men and women moved around a field where Franco's body had been found. Shot three times, then abandoned. His government-issued vehicle apparently stolen by one of Sam Luciano's known associates. A man whose body was recently discovered in a similar condition after his image was released by local news channels.

A deep sigh poured from Maisy's chest. So it was true. The marshal sent to transport her was dead. She'd expected as much, but the news felt exceptionally devastating anyway.

Blaze squeezed her hand. "You okay?"

"No. I keep thinking that this started for me when Luciano killed Natalie and Aaron. Then I wouldn't stop pushing until he'd been tracked down and put behind bars, awaiting trial. Now, because we did that, because I wanted justice for those two deaths, he has killed the marshal sent to pick me up, Clara, two other witnesses and the original hit man." Her breath shuddered out of her. "That's five more dead because I wanted justice for two. If he wasn't awaiting trial, there wouldn't be a need for witnesses. And he wouldn't be killing them."

"This isn't your fault," Blaze reminded her. "Luciano is a killer. His body count would be much higher if he was free. And if you weren't willing to testify, to make sure he winds up in a maximum-security prison, his body count would never end."

Maisy knew that was true, but she hated what was happening anyway and feared where the ripple effect would go next. "I'm worried for the prosecutor's safety," she said. "And for Dr. Nazir. What if she loses her life over this, too? Just because she's the unlucky doctor Clara and I picked to monitor my pregnancy." She pushed away from Blaze so she could look into his face. "Whoever tried to run me over yesterday knew she was my doctor."

His sharp gray eyes searched hers until she could nearly see their thoughts aligning. "And the driver knew when you'd be there."

"But you'd just moved that appointment up a day before," she said. "How is that possible?"

"I wondered about that, too," he said. "And I passed the question on to Derek, Maxwell and

Isaac. There were a handful of lawmen outside my cabin with me when I called to move the appointment. Any one of them could have overheard me."

"Or…" Maisy's shoulders tensed, and her lips parted. A terrifying new possibility registered. "Is it possible your phone is tapped?" If so, could they use the tap to track them? Were they in danger? Even here on a mountaintop?

Blaze shook his head. "No. I've checked it thoroughly. The phone's not bugged, but someone was listening that day. I called the personal number Nazir gave us while you were sleeping and asked her if there were any new employees at her office. It was a long shot, but I worried Luciano could have gotten an ally hired. She assured me there were no new hires."

Maisy relaxed by a fraction. She'd imagined the planted employee hurting her doctor if Luciano gave the order, and the thought sent shards of ice through her veins. "Good."

"Yes and no," he said. "Honestly, the leak could still have come from the doctor's office. Anyone can be bought for the right price, because everyone has a weak spot. If Luciano or his goon figured out who your doctor was, he could easily have bribed or blackmailed someone who's worked there for years."

"Everyone's a suspect," she groaned. "I'd be

mad, but I know that once our baby is born, I'd do anything to protect her."

Blaze pressed a kiss against the back of her hand, still twined with his. Then another on her bump. "There's also the possibility no one at Nazir's office is dirty. And none of the men on site at my place overheard me change the appointment. There aren't a lot of obstetricians in the county where your safe house was situated. Some quick deduction would narrow the options once Luciano's men saw that you were pregnant. Being as far along as you are, and knowing you were in the cabin when it was smoke bombed, maybe the office was simply being staked out."

"Assuming I'd show up for a proper exam," she said.

"Maybe. But regardless of the course of events that brought us here, we're going to be okay," he promised. "The trial is less than a week away. Prosecution is alive and well, as far as I've heard. And we still have two witnesses. So the weight of Luciano's trial isn't completely on your shoulders. Maxwell or the marshals could still get one of the men who broke into my house to turn on him. Our case can only get stronger. All hope isn't lost yet."

His phone dinged with an incoming text message, and he shifted away from her to grab the device. A second notification dinged as he released her hand to enter the password on his lock screen. The sound came a third time as he frowned at the screen.

Maisy stroked his lean, sinewy forearm while he read, thankful for his presence and the hope he continually provided. Especially when she was feeling hopeless.

Blaze was right, of course. She wasn't in this alone. There was still another witness and known associates who might talk in exchange for leniency.

Blaze muttered under his breath as he scrolled. The crease in his brow confirmed the news wasn't good. He typed. Then swore.

"What?" she whispered, unable to wait any longer. If the new killer had found them, she wasn't sure she had enough luck or stamina to survive another attack.

Blaze turned the phone's screen in her direction, revealing the image of a police report apparently photographed then shared with him by text.

"Death report," Maisy said, chest tightening as she scanned the record for details, trying to place the name. "Kelly Hartman?"

"Yeah." Blaze dropped the phone into his lap, then pressed one hand across his forehead. "She was the other witness."

Chapter Fifteen

Maisy's hands began to shake. A tremor beat its way through her as she watched Blaze typing on his laptop at the little table. He'd called his brother, then his sergeant, searching for more information about Kelly Hartman's death. He'd been at the dinette for the better part of an hour, but Maisy couldn't move. Fear had glued her in place.

The other shoe had dropped, and it was a pattern she'd grown to hate. Each time she let herself believe the daily horror and tragedy had reached its end, something like this reminded her the situation would only end one of two ways—with her dead or Luciano in supermax. Maisy was doing all she could to make it the latter.

The thought of her death hollowed her, and she wrapped protective arms around her middle, rejecting the possibility. If she died, her baby died, and Maisy would not allow that.

Blaze's gaze flicked to Maisy as he pushed upright and rubbed his jaw. He tucked his cell phone into the pocket of his hoodie as he returned to her side. "Sorry, that took longer than I expected."

He exhaled long and slow as he lowered onto the cushion beside her. His legs stretched out before him. His shoulders drooped with fatigue, and his eyes were burdened. "It seems that Kelly Hartman was a longtime girlfriend of Luciano," he said. "She was also the mother to two of his children. Someone from her staff found her body this morning inside her Nashville home."

"Shot?" Maisy asked. Three bullets seemed to be the theme.

"No. The initial report listed her cause of death as an overdose. Her blood alcohol level was high, and there were a number of prescription drugs in her system, though none of those had been prescribed to her. The children's au pair claimed Kelly rarely had more than a single glass of wine and didn't take any medications outside the occasional aspirin or antihistamine. But there's speculation that Luciano's imprisonment and upcoming trial had worn on her in ways she hadn't let on outwardly." He scrubbed his jaw again. "The coroner will know more in a few days, but the timing makes it hard for me to think she's dead for any reason other than Luciano ordered it."

Maisy stared, nearly choked with disbelief. "I can't believe he'd kill the mother of his children." Her stomach pitched and turned at the thought. Was Luciano even human?

"He didn't do it with his own hands," Blaze said, "but he most likely pulled the trigger, figuratively speaking."

"How old are the kids?" Maisy asked, not sure she really wanted to know. Knowing would only make the facts harder to process.

"Seven and ten."

"Those poor children," Maisy said, feeling the weight of their loss on her heart. "What happens to them now? Will they be handed over to Luciano if he gets out of jail? Raised by a murderous monster?"

"I don't know," Blaze said. "Maybe."

"What if he's sent to supermax?"

Blaze considered the question a moment before answering. "The children would be better off in nearly anyone else's care," Blaze said. "So that wouldn't be a bad thing for them. Chances are good that Kelly had family who will want them. Fighting for custody should be easy given Luciano's lengthy criminal record, even if he's set free. Which he won't be.

Because we're going to do everything we can to keep that from happening."

Maisy's heart fell impossibly further for the children she'd never met. There wouldn't be a happy ending for them. "I'll bet that if anyone tries to take Luciano's children, he'll unleash the full power of his money and influence to stop it from happening. Assuming he doesn't just kill the potential guardians and be done with it," she said. "In which case, the kids will go through yet another unthinkable loss."

Blaze pursed his lips, presumably in agreement.

"Did you learn anything else?" Maisy forced her mind away from Luciano's children.

"A little." He nodded. "Maxwell said local police responded to a break-in at the Hartman home last week. The family was out, but the security alarm was triggered. The intruder wasn't caught. Nothing appeared missing or disturbed. Could be nothing, but again, timing."

"Last week," Maisy said. "So, the initial breech at Kelly's place came before the attack on my safe house."

"By two days," Blaze said. "Could be that the first hit man struck out in Nashville, so he made his way to Kentucky."

"Making his rounds," she mused, numb and

horrified. "Picking off witnesses." She dragged her fingers across her collarbone, a series of new questions forming in her mind. "Why do you think Kelly was willing to testify against Luciano? Why now? And why wasn't she in witness protection? She, of all people, would know how dangerous he is."

"I asked the lead prosecutor, Jack Hisey, the same thing. He said that when she initially came to him, she thought vanishing into protective custody would tip off Luciano or one of his goons. She didn't have regular contact with her ex, but she believed someone was watching her, likely a henchman," Blaze said. "She thought it best to behave as if nothing out of the ordinary was about to happen."

"That had to be awful," Maisy said. "Knowing the father of her children was the kind of man Luciano is, and feeling as if he had someone watching everything she did." She shivered at the thought.

"She was right," Blaze said, "or that's my take, anyway. Hisey said her initial split from Luciano was a mutual decision. Then she got comfortable in her new life and went on a date. It was her first and last. Her suitor was in a serious car accident on his way home. He's in a wheelchair now. That was nearly four years after leaving Luciano."

Maisy's mouth fell open. She took a minute to let that sink in. Four years of believing he'd let her go. Four years of believing her life was her own. And that was how he'd shown her she was wrong. By trying to kill a man she went on one date with. "I don't know how anything shocks me anymore, but I wasn't expecting that."

"Psychopaths like Luciano tend to be territorial," Blaze said. "Women and children are pawns to them. Equivalent to property. It's unlikely he even views them as human. They are things to own, sell, trade or dispose of as he sees fit. And there is no expiration date on that claim."

Maisy grimaced. "I don't know how you can make a career of this. Surrounded by the ugliest parts of humanity every day. How do you have any hope left at all?"

"It's not all bad, and not every day," he said, managing a feeble smile. "I see good things happen, too. Like when an abused child or spouse finds their footing after trauma and rises above it. I help put killers behind bars. Find justice for victims and punishment for the criminals. If I've helped even one person in the years I've been doing this, then any amount of frustration or heartache I've endured has been worth it."

A spark of wonder and respect formed in Maisy. If Luciano was the epitome of evil, Blaze was the definition of good. Then, Kelly came back to mind, and the positive feeling stretched to cover her, as well. "Knowing all that he was capable of, she was still willing to testify. That's incredibly brave."

"I agree."

"I can probably answer my own question from before," Maisy said, realizing the thing that had been right in front of her. "Kelly chose to testify against him now and not sooner because this is the first time he's been in jail, with a murder trial coming and three others willing to testify." She knew this was her chance to help put him away for good. She wasn't alone in the fight. "Once he's in the supermax prison, he wouldn't have the same reach or control over her. This was her chance at real freedom for her and her children."

"The odds were definitely in her favor with four of you slated to take the stand," Blaze said.

Maisy longed to scream in frustration at the injustice of it all. "How is this happening?" she asked. "We're less than a week from trial, and the case against him is being completely dismantled one witness at a time. I can't decide if it's ironic or just really on the nose that a murderer is going to get off his murder charges by having the witnesses murdered." She dragged angry hands through her hair, digging deep against her skull and curling her fingers into the soft brown locks. "How can a man behind bars have this kind of impact on the outside world?"

"County lockup isn't exactly Fort Knox. He's allowed phone calls and visitors. The contact is monitored, but permitted nonetheless. And Luciano's smart enough not to say or do anything we can use against him. Which is why we want to see him reassigned to Cumberland, preferably for life."

Maisy considered the phone calls and visitors. "Can you check the jail's logs to see who he's been in contact with, then question them? Maybe one of those people is the hit man, or at least the middleman passing the orders."

"Maxwell's already looking," Blaze said.

She drummed her fingers on her bump. West Liberty's police force was good at what they did. She remembered that from when they'd helped her before, following Natalie's death.

Blaze curved a protective arm around her shoulders and tugged her close. "We're going to get through this," he promised.

"We have to," she said quietly. "All these lost lives can't be for nothing. Kelly's children, and Clara's, all have to grow up without their mother because of him. There has to be something we can do before he hurts anyone else."

"Not tonight," he said. "Tonight we obey Dr. Nazir and try to relax. I'll keep tabs on the case. You should try to rest. Tomorrow, we'll set an appointment with the prosecutor."

BLAZE OPENED THE door for Derek early the next morning. A gust of icy wind blew him inside, curling Blaze's bare toes against the chilly wooden floorboards.

"Hello, brother," Derek said, another box of doughnuts in hand with a pint of mint chocolate chip ice cream on top. "Clever hideout."

"Thanks." Blaze tucked the ice cream into the freezer, then grabbed a pair of mugs from the dish rack. "No pickles?"

Derek shrugged, helping himself to a mug and the freshly brewed coffee. "I didn't like the selection at the general store. I asked the man behind the counter if he'd seen you. He said he had." He lifted the steaming mug to his lips, one eyebrow pulled high. "He described you both to a tee."

Blaze took a bear claw from the doughnut box, then bit into it to stifle a curse. "I knew we spent too long in there."

"He thought Maisy was a 'lovely young

lady.'" Derek formed air quotes around the description.

Blaze felt his jaw lock. He'd been reckless shopping there. He should've gone to a big box store in another county, someplace with a thousand shoppers that no one remembered.

"At least you paid in cash," Derek said. "He remembered that, too. You didn't use a credit card to check in here, did you?"

"Of course not."

"Well, you did shop at the only store on the mountain," Derek challenged. "Register under false identities?"

"Yeah, and I went into the lodge's office alone. I pretended to be an artist, traveling from out of state."

Derek nodded. "That's good. Hopefully Maisy didn't say too much to the guy at the general store."

"She wouldn't." Blaze refilled his mug, then motioned Derek to have a seat with him at the table. "But we should probably set up a false trail. There are only five days left until the trial." He sipped the bitter pick-me-up, ordering his brain to kick in with a plan. Something to misdirect anyone searching for her. "Why don't I send one of my credit cards with you?" he suggested. "You can make a few purchases. Create a false trail for us. You and I look enough alike to fool anyone who doesn't know us." Despite a distinct difference in eye color, anyone not looking too closely could easily make the mistake. "Get cash from ATMs. Pay for gas somewhere. Buy groceries."

"Pickles?" Derek asked, a cocky grin on his face, palm open in acceptance of Blaze's offer.

"Anything you want. Keep the receipts." He smiled. "Why don't you trade me cars when you leave? That'll help sell it if the tracker asks about my vehicle, or gets a look at a surveillance feed." He fished a rarely used card from his wallet and passed it to his brother.

Derek smacked his lips. "You've been after my truck since the day I drove it off the lot."

Blaze laughed. The unexpected sound vibrated through him. "You got me."

Derek pocketed the credit card, looking a lot less happy about shopping with the card when his truck would be in Blaze's care. "How's Maisy holding up?"

"Better than me, I think," Blaze admitted. "She's always been formidable, but the pregnancy seems to have fortified her. I'd almost feel bad for anyone trying to harm her now."

"Well, there's at least one guy at the county hospital who'd agree," Derek said, a thick smirk in his tone. "The guy she hit with Nana's frying pan is still under observation."

Blaze grinned. "She's only five weeks from delivery, and the sky is falling around her. I have to keep reminding myself I've just got to get her through the next few days, and her life will become incomprehensibly simpler." He tried not to think about how different things would be a week from now. A month. A year. Not yet. Now was the time to concentrate. One thing at a time. First, lie low. Then, the trial. After that, he'd see if she still wanted him the way he'd always wanted her.

Was it possible that she might? Even when she didn't need him anymore? And if so, for how long? It had been his experience that women rarely tolerated sharing him with his job, and being a detective was a 24-7 gig. He was never truly off the clock. And to be honest, he didn't want to be. He needed someone who understood that and supported him in the choice. The same way he would support her on whatever she wanted in return.

"I'm here to help," Derek said. "At your disposal. Don't forget that."

Blaze rubbed his unshaven chin. "I know, and I appreciate it. Maisy's the last witness standing. Luciano's man is going to be working hard to silence her. Her doctor tasked me with keeping her calm and rested. She's concerned about preterm labor." He dropped his hand in a moment of total candor. "I'm a wreck, man."

Derek set his coffee mug aside, eyes narrowing. "I would be, too. There's a lot at stake here."

"Everything is at stake here," Blaze corrected.

Derek kicked back on his chair, arms crossed and jaw clenched. "I hate that the two of you are going through this. I think about you and your situation a lot, and, honestly, I don't know what I'd do in your position."

Blaze rolled his shoulders forward, resting his forearms on the table. He clasped his fingers and counted his breaths, trying to rein back the surge of desperation. "Every time I think we're going to get through this safely, there's another attack or someone else is murdered. I feel like we're in an out-of-control car without seat belts. I'm trying to keep it together for her and the baby, but I can't sleep. Can't eat. Can't concentrate. And none of that is good. Especially not right now."

"Good morning." Maisy's voice snapped Blaze onto his feet.

His neck and ears burned, and he prayed she hadn't heard his confession. He'd tell her all about his fears and feelings of ineptitude someday, when this was behind them, if she wanted.

Right now, he needed her to believe she was safe and that he could keep her that way. Partly to manage her stress level, but mostly because as long as Maisy still believed in him, Blaze could keep believing in himself.

"What's going on?" she asked, gaze circling suspiciously from brother to brother.

"Derek brought doughnuts and ice cream." Blaze smiled, then waved an open hand in his brother's direction.

"Yep," he agreed casually, shooting Blaze a pointed look. He flipped open the lid on the doughnut box, then turned a smile on Maisy. "I hope you like bear claws and cream sticks."

She grinned, already headed toward the table and the open pastry box. "Morning," she said softly to Blaze as she selected a fritter. A tiny smile curved her mouth as she glided past him to an empty chair.

His heart ached with the need to protect her, and with the utter helplessness he felt in the face of an unnamed enemy. At least when Maisy had arrived on his doorstep, she'd seen the safe house shooter. They'd had something to go on, someone to look for. Now, he had no idea who was after her. "Can I make you some tea?" he asked, setting a hand against the small of her back.

"That would be great. Thank you." She took

the seat beside Derek, then fixed him with a scrutinizing stare. "You didn't come all the way out here to bring me doughnuts, did you?"

Derek shifted in her direction, slinging an arm across the back of his chair. "I'm also checking up on my little brother and future niece or nephew."

Maisy set a napkin on her bump, then watched Derek as she took a bite of the fritter.

Blaze returned with her tea.

"Do you also come bearing news?" Maisy asked Derek.

"'Fraid not." Derek straightened in his seat, looking genuinely remorseful.

"Making any progress on identifying the leak in law enforcement?" she asked.

Blaze shook his head. Negative.

Maisy refocused on her tea and fritter, looking a little deflated after the brief exchange.

Derek's expression brightened. "Everyone's pointing fingers, though. The cops are blaming the marshals, since the safe house shooter was masquerading as one of them. The marshals think someone at the police department tipped the shooter off about the transport. The guys at the PD have a pool going on which agency has the mole. So far, most of the police force is leaning toward the marshals, but there's growing interest in the warden at county lockup.

Everyone has their own reasons and theories. Maxwell keeps demanding they knock it off." He pulled a stick of gum from his pocket, unwrapping it with a grin. "Bets are unprofessional and distracting. I've got my money on the guard. It wasn't an option in the poll, so all I've got to win or lose is pride."

Maisy rolled her eyes. "Good thing you have a little of that to spare."

Blaze laughed, enjoying the easy dynamic.

Derek stuffed the gum into his mouth, then neatly folded the wrapper. "Any chance you might want to move this party closer to the courthouse?"

"Why?" Maisy asked, as Blaze gave a firm "No."

Derek's attention flicked to Blaze. "If not today, then sometime before the trial. The drive to West Liberty from here provides too many opportunities for an ambush, especially the morning of the trial, when you're expected to come out of hiding."

Maisy's ivory skin paled impossibly further. "An ambush?"

Derek lifted a palm, then lowered it to the table. "I'm just trying to troubleshoot."

Blaze reached for Maisy's hand, and she easily turned her palm to his, linking their fingers.

Derek's eyes flashed over the familiar touch,

then locked on Blaze. "Have you spoken to the prosecutor?"

"Yeah. A few times since Kelly Hartman's body was found. We're meeting with him tomorrow."

"Opposing counsel rejected the suggestion of a livestream testimony?" Derek guessed.

"They haven't responded," Blaze said. "But now that we're down another witness, Hisey's going to present the possibility to the judge again. Kelly's death was made to appear self-inflicted, but even the possibility her overdose was murder should motivate Judge Wise to accept our request. The prosecution also plans to suggest we enter a video recording of Maisy's testimony as evidence and have it played for the jury instead of any live interaction. Honestly, I prefer that to anything else. The more space I can put between her and this trial, the better."

Derek nodded. "Surely no one can argue that."

"Oh, they can," Blaze assured. "And they will. I'm certain of it. Luciano's legal team won't lie down that easily. They're going to be ready for a fight."

Maisy's thin fingers tightened on Blaze's, and he stroked the back of her hand with his thumb. "I can take the stand," she assured. "I've come this far. I can finish this."

"I know you can," Blaze said, swaddling her hand in his. "And I'm going to keep you safe while you do."

Chapter Sixteen

Maisy was strapped into Blaze's borrowed truck and headed back down the mountain at precisely three o'clock the next day. The truck was enormous, with an extended cab and dual rear wheels. She would've felt invincible inside the beast, but it barely seemed to fit on the winding resort roads and didn't match much better with the suddenly narrow highway lanes.

She fiddled with the chipping paint on her fingernails, unexpectedly nervous. She'd waited for what felt like an eternity to get to this point. Four days left until the trial. The ball was in motion and picking up speed. The reality of it all was nearly overwhelming. The end was finally in sight.

She'd spent an hour choosing an outfit to meet the prosecutor, not that there was much left in her maternity wardrobe that still fit comfortably. Her bump seemed to have doubled in size these last few weeks. She wanted to look as trustworthy and believable as possible if she got the chance to video record her testimony today. A cream tunic top and black leggings had been the winning ensemble. Simple. Presentable. Forgettable. If the recording was seen by a jury, she didn't want them to remember her clothing. She wanted them to remember her words. She'd wrapped a simple black ribbon around her hair like a headband and worn the earrings Natalie had given her at college graduation for luck. Her mother's book, the one that had started it all, was inside her handbag. The Daniels women were all represented today. Right down to the sweet baby girl inside her.

Blaze had dressed casually, in jeans and a gray V-neck sweater, the collar of a white T-shirt barely visible beneath. He'd paired that with his black bomber jacket and leather boots. The overall look was enticing. The intense concentration on his face was borderline lethal. She could only imagine what he was thinking, and she didn't feel brave enough to ask. He'd confirmed the appointment after breakfast, using the attorney's personal email account. Blaze said he couldn't be sure the office phones weren't tapped, so email was better. Silent. And the account was never used for business.

Her baby kicked, and Maisy placed a palm against her abdomen, eager to feel the little movement once more. She rested her head against the seat as she waited, watching snow-dusted trees and rooftops zip past the foggy window.

Blaze's repetitive gaze heated her cheeks, probably working out everything that could go wrong, and how to troubleshoot it.

She turned to offer him a small smile. "Everything okay?"

"I was going to ask you the same thing. More contractions?"

"No." She caressed her bump. "Just a few kicks."

"Okay." His gaze dipped briefly to her lips, and a blast of memory rushed over her.

They'd shared another amazingly intimate and possibly stupid night together. One she'd shamelessly enjoyed every second of and was certain never to forget.

Despite her bulbous shape and the forty pounds she'd gained, Blaze somehow still thought she was beautiful. Sexy, smart and fierce. He told her as much, fervently and often. He claimed he saw sensual curves where she saw added weight. Most importantly, he saw her. Just like he always had.

She swept her gaze away from him, hopeful but unsure. She'd read about men with hero complexes while she'd been stuck at the safe house, wondering if what she and Blaze had shared could've been real. According to her research, some men in professions like his were addicted to the thrill of saving lives, of swooping in and being the big, tough protector. What would happen when she didn't need that anymore?

Did he truly love her? Or was he simply enamored by her constant need for protection?

The truck rocked over a pothole as Blaze made the final turn into town, returning Maisy's attention to the moment. Emergency lights slashed through the sky near the courthouse, and a crowd gathered on the sidewalks outside.

"What's going on?" she asked, straining to identify the cause of the commotion.

Blaze frowned. "I don't know." He powered the window down as they arrived in the thick of the congestion, then stretched an arm outside, motioning to a uniformed officer.

The man's brows rose, and a smile bloomed in recognition. He jogged to a stop outside Blaze's window. "What are you doing here?" he asked. "Everyone's been looking for you."

"I'm not here," Blaze said, pausing to let the point settle in.

The other man's eyes flicked to Maisy, then back. He dipped his chin once in acknowledgment.

"What's going on?" Blaze asked.

The younger cop rocked back on his heels. "Someone took a shot at Judge Wise. He's fine, but the rest of the building's staff is a mess."

Maisy's heart pounded against her ribs. She knew that name.

"He's set to preside over Luciano's trial next week," Blaze said.

"Yeah, and he's ticked." The cop grinned. "Wise said he refuses to be intimidated by a criminal. The trial won't be moved or delayed."

She pressed a palm to her sternum, trying to remain calm. Her gaze drifted carefully over the faces in the crowd. Across nearby buildings, streets and windows, searching for signs of a shooter.

"How'd someone get a gun past security?" Blaze asked.

"Didn't," the cop said. "There was an anonymous tip about a bomb, and they evacuated. The shot came after everyone was outside. I heard it as I got here. Pure chaos. Scared everyone except Wise. It just made him angry."

"Anyone get a look at the gunman?"

"No, and get this." The cop leaned closer, his voice low. "This is the second bomb scare in two days. Luciano's going all out to postpone this trial. Best part is that nothing's working. His time's nearly up, and he knows it."

Maisy started at the blast of a whistle.

The crowd outside began to move back through the courthouse doors.

"Guess I'm done here," the cop said, nodding at Blaze, then tipping his hat to Maisy. "Stay safe. You're almost to the finish line."

Blaze powered up his window, sealing the icy air outside once more.

Maisy tracked the exiting man with her eyes. "How well do you know him?" she asked. What if he was the dirty lawman? He could be on his way to tip off Luciano or the hit man. *He could be the hit man.* "Do you trust him?"

"That's Van," Blaze answered, rolling slowly forward with traffic. "And yes, I do. I trained him when he joined the force last year."

Maisy concentrated on her breathing and tried not to remember her previous talk with Blaze. The one where they'd established that anyone could be bought or blackmailed.

He parked Derek's massive truck in a small lot outside the historic brick building, then ushered Maisy quickly inside.

Staffers and guests filed through security,

then scattered on the other side, hurrying across the wide marble floors, down hallways and into offices. Their expressions were wary, the tension palpable.

Maisy waited anxiously as Blaze flashed his badge at a guard with salt-and-pepper hair and deep russet-colored skin. "I hear you've had quite a day," Blaze said.

The guard motioned them through the gate, then split his attention between Blaze and the continued flow of incomers. A silver name badge identified him as Terrance Moreland. "Yesterday folks were afraid there was a bomb," Terrance said. "Today they're worried about a bomb and a shooter. What's tomorrow going to bring?" He trailed a curious gaze over Maisy.

She lifted her fingers in a nervous wave.

"How's Judge Wise doing?" Blaze asked, redirecting Terrance's attention.

He laughed. "Wise is one tough old bird." He motioned the next man through the gate. "He wasn't hit. Says he'll wear a bulletproof vest if he has to, but he won't let a criminal corrupt the justice system. Poor stenographer, though. She was so shaken, she took a medical leave until the trial ends. She was standing with Wise when the shot came. Bullet lodged in the brick, not two feet away."

Maisy watched the thinning crowd, thoughts torn. She liked the idea of a judge unwilling to be bullied by Luciano, but felt equally awful for the woman who'd taken a leave to deal with the threat. Then a new worry formed. "Who will replace the stenographer?" And how could anyone be sure that person wasn't a plant?

Terrance's brows rose. His eyes fixed on Maisy.

She regretted the question immediately. He'd barely noticed her until she'd opened her mouth.

"We'll let you get back to work," Blaze said, offering Terrance his hand for a shake.

He accepted, then turned back to the men and women moving through the gate.

Blaze set a hand against the small of her back, then guided her down the nearest hall. "Everyone who enters the courtroom that day will be thoroughly vetted," he assured quietly. "We all know what's riding on this case, and the lengths Luciano will go to get away with murder."

Maisy shivered. She could only hope the killer wouldn't really blow up the courthouse if that was what it took to stop the trial.

BLAZE ESCORTED MAISY into the prosecutor's office. The waiting room was vacant, the receptionist's expression expectant. "There you are," she said, rising with a warm smile. "Right on time despite the chaos."

"Hi, Karen." He hugged her, then stepped back to introduce Maisy. Karen had been one of his mother's friends for as long as he could remember. "Is Jack ready to see us?"

"I'm sure he is," she said, returning to her seat. "Just give me a minute, and I'll let him know you're here." She pressed a few numbers on her telephone then announced into the speaker that his four o'clock appointment had arrived. "He's been in there preparing all day."

When Hisey's closed door didn't immediately open, Blaze motioned Maisy to a pair of seats in the farthest corner of the room. Seats with clear views of every door and window. "I've been thinking we should request your testimony be recorded, regardless of how the judge and other attorneys respond to our request. Having a taped account on hand is smart. Just in case."

The office phone rang, and Karen answered. Her sudden smile suggested it was a personal call.

"What does that mean?" Maisy whispered, drawing his attention back to her wide hazel eyes. She'd wrapped thin arms around her middle again. "Do you mean, in case I'm dead?"

Blaze blinked. His heart plummeted at the suggestion, and it took him a moment to understand her question. "No!" he hissed, stunned at her interpretation. "Of course not." His whisper cracked like a whip through the nearly silent room. "I meant, in case you can't make it to trial because it becomes too dangerous to be here in person." He rubbed his brow, struggling to make sense of Maisy's reaction.

Her wide eyes narrowed. "If the trial moves forward, I have to be there. Otherwise there was never a purpose for any of this. The chaos. The deaths. The only reason to send a recording in my place is if I can't be there, and I can only think of one reason for that."

Blaze felt his temperature rise, and he locked it down. "I know that's what you want, and I'll do my best to get you there, but Maisy," he said, pausing to search her face, allowing her to search his, "I won't knowingly endanger your life and the life of our baby."

Her lips flattened into a thin white line, and heat flashed across her beautiful face. "Judge Wise isn't letting Luciano keep him from presiding over this trial, and I won't let Luciano stop me from testifying. It's the right thing to do, and I've waited half a year to do it."

"I don't care what Judge Wise does," Blaze said, holding tightly to his calm. "His risks don't matter to me. Yours do. I'm here to protect you."

Her ivory skin turned pink as she leaned in his direction, expression hard. "You don't care what the judge does because his loss doesn't impact your life. Does that mean his life doesn't matter? That it's somehow less valuable than mine?"

"To me," Blaze said, his words rushing out. "Yes."

Maisy's angry expression fell into something strangely blank. She caressed her bump, quieted by his outburst and offering no rebuttal. The fire had gone out of her eyes, replaced by something like shock or confusion.

Silence gonged around them, and a quick look in Karen's direction confirmed she'd heard the exchange. She was still on the call, but her eyes had fixed on Blaze.

He checked his watch, then stretched upright, eager to get their appointment over with and return Maisy to the safety of the cabin. At least there, they could talk about this without fear of another bomb scare or whatever else might happen next at the courthouse.

He strode back to Karen, then waited for her to disconnect her call. They'd already waited ten minutes past Maisy's scheduled time with Hisey. Given her situation, it was hard to believe he hadn't rushed her inside the minute Karen announced her arrival. "What did he say when you told him we were here?" Blaze asked, tipping his head in the direction of the lawyer's closed office door.

She stared from behind large round-framed glasses, her sleek silver bob tucked behind her ears. "Nothing, but I'm sure he'll only be another minute. He's been awaiting Miss Daniels's arrival all day and preparing for it all week. He didn't even leave during the bomb scare this time."

"Oh no." Maisy's whisper reached his ears easily, raising the hairs on his arms to attention. She drifted to his side and reached for his hand.

Blaze squeezed her fingers briefly, hoping to convey reassurance before releasing her in favor of his sidearm. "When was the last time you spoke to him?" he asked Karen.

"This morning. He brought in scones and lattes, then told me to hold his calls and visitors until you arrived. Where are you going?"

Blaze curled his fingers over his weapon's grip as he headed for Hisey's closed door. He rapped his knuckles against the heavy wood. "Hisey?"

"Someone took a shot at the judge during

the evacuation today," Maisy said from behind him, much closer than she should be.

"What does that have to do with Jack?" Karen asked.

"Hopefully nothing." Blaze rested a hand on the knob and gave it a slow turn.

"Attorney Hisey wouldn't shoot anyone," Karen said. "This doesn't make any sense."

"That's not what we're suggesting," Maisy said.

Not at all, Blaze thought, pulling his gun and swinging the door wide.

The scream that followed was Karen's.

Jack Hisey was slumped behind his desk, a gunshot wound in his forehead.

Chapter Seventeen

Maisy curled on the couch with her mother's book the next morning. She hadn't slept well after the stress of finding the lead prosecutor's body, but she was slowly making up for the lost z's with naps and easing her nerves with tea. She and Blaze hadn't talked about what he'd said in the attorney's office, that her life meant more to him than the judge's. Instead, Hisey's death had consumed him.

Blaze had worked the rest of the day and into the night, bringing the prosecution's B-team up to speed and coordinating the replacement materials needed for the trial. Whoever had killed Hisey—while the rest of the building's employees had blazed a trail to the sidewalk— had also taken every paper file and scrap of evidence on Luciano. Putting an even larger, albeit temporary dent in the case.

The trial was just three days away, and Maisy had no idea what to expect, or if she'd have the opportunity to prepare. Everyone involved was in a frenzy, scrambling to pick up the torch for Hisey and carry on, but time was slipping away. It was hard not to worry. Judge Wise had refused another postponement, despite the loss of lead counsel. He rightly claimed that these tragedies would continue to happen until Luciano was sentenced, and putting off the trial would only lead to more unnecessary deaths. Whatever Luciano thought could keep him out of supermax.

Blaze and his brother reviewed the case details from the cabin's little kitchen–turned–makeshift war room. Derek had slept over, not that either man appeared to have actually slept. They'd fretted through dinner over the prosecution's mission to find a replacement for Hisey. Someone brave enough to oppose Luciano and tenacious enough to get up to speed in three days, when Hisey had been preparing for half a year. Maisy had called it a night by eleven, emotionally and mentally exhausted beyond measure.

A hoot of victory turned her on the cushion for a peek into the kitchen. Derek had set up a printer on the countertop, and the cabinet doors were covered in papers, maps, photos and sticky notes. Two laptops, empty coffee mugs and takeout containers cluttered the small dinette. "What?" she asked, a bubble of hope forming inside her. It was the first happy sound she'd heard in a long while.

Blaze moved in her direction, latching broad hands over the back of the couch and smiling. "They found a replacement for Hisey. A law professor named Julia Struthers. She hasn't practiced in two years, but her record before moving to the classroom was impeccable. She's at the prosecutor's office now, familiarizing herself with the details of the case. Maxwell's meeting with her in an hour to supply anything she needs from local PD, and she has a similar meeting with the marshals first thing tomorrow."

A smile opened Maisy's mouth, and she felt a weight lifting from her shoulders. "That's fantastic."

He nodded, a small grin spreading across his lips. "It's a good start."

"There's more?" she guessed.

"She's coming here to talk to you today," he said. "There's no time to waste. I'm picking her up in Derek's truck from a café in the next town. She won't be announced publicly as Hisey's replacement until the evening news, so our chances of going unnoticed are good. She'll be home with a security detail before the cat's out of the bag. And you'll be here, safe."

A mix of emotions spun in Maisy's heart and head. "So, you're leaving me here while you get her?" She looked past him to Derek who snorted in the kitchen.

"Derek's staying with you," Blaze said. "I think he's right about us becoming a target on the road, if we were spotted and identified. You're safest here, so that's where we want to keep you. At least for a few more days. Derek can protect you."

She cast another look in Blaze's brother's direction. Derek was a well-respected P.I., sharing a private practice with their cousin. He wasn't an official lawman, but he was undeniably tough, if a little reckless, but smart and fast, too. He would undoubtedly defend her and their baby, probably to the death if needed. There was something about these Winchesters and their need to be heroes. "Okay, but how can you be sure Julia Struthers isn't being bribed or blackmailed to intentionally throw the case? Or to gain access to me and…you know…" She formed a finger gun with one hand, and Blaze quickly covered it with a gentle palm.

"Julia has agreed to a pat down, so I can check for wires and weapons. She'll power off her cell phone to stop digital tracking and allow me to examine it for signs of listening devices. She fully understands what's happening here and why the precautions are necessary. She's eager to see Luciano's reign of terror stopped and would probably agree to anything that made us feel safe."

"Wow." Maisy nodded, a smile forming. "Okay, then."

He laughed. "That was exactly the way I felt when I spoke with her." Blaze leaned over the couch and kissed the top of Maisy's head. "Refresher on your tea?"

"Sure."

"Getting hungry yet?" He accepted the empty mug with tented brows.

"No." Her stomach had been queasy since they'd returned to the cabin yesterday. Anxiety, she supposed, and she was doing her best to emotionally disengage from the trauma, for her baby's sake. High blood pressure wasn't something she could afford to develop this late in her pregnancy.

Blaze watched her carefully, as if trying to read her mind. He thankfully relented without further questions. She didn't want to talk about the nausea, or the Braxton-Hicks contractions that had nearly brought her to tears after breakfast. She could handle those things on her own, by following Dr. Nazir's prescription for rest. Blaze needed to stay focused.

Maisy excused herself to freshen up when Blaze left to meet Julia Struthers.

Derek eyed her suspiciously as she made the announcement, but he only smiled and said he'd be there if she needed anything.

She curled on her bed and fought a budding sense of panic until she fell unexpectedly back to sleep.

Her eyes opened at the sounds of a vehicle outside. The engine was too quiet to be Derek's diesel truck returning, and the sound of a closing car door nearly caused Maisy's heart to seize. Images of the impostor marshal who'd killed Clara flashed through her mind. "Derek?" she called, swinging her feet over the edge of the bed. "Derek?"

His lithe footfalls sounded softly outside her open door. "It's fine, but stay here." He held her gaze a beat longer, then vanished, back toward the living room.

She followed, unable to stop herself. There wasn't a back door near the bedroom. If Derek was taken by a killer, she'd have no means of escape there. The cabin was designed with two points of entry. A front door and a back door. One in the living room. The other in the kitchen. Both were down the hallway where Derek had disappeared.

He stood at the front window, staring at

something outside, and glanced her way when she approached. "Blaze warned me that you don't follow instructions well."

She shoved her feet into sneakers as memories of her last harrowing escape grew more vivid and terrifying. Her limbs twitched, ready to run.

"Looks like one of the resort's trucks," Derek said, his attention fixed beyond the glass once more. "Snowplow on the front. Resort logo on the side. The guy got out and started shoveling debris out of the ditch across the road. He's wearing a reflective jacket, coveralls, work boots. Fits the right visual." He lifted his cell phone to the window and snapped a photo.

"Sure," Maisy said flatly. "And the man who came for me at the safe house was wearing a marshal jacket. Driving the real marshal's government-issued vehicle." Her voice quaked with the words. Clara's killer had taken what he needed after murdering the marshal. For all she knew, a resort worker could be dead somewhere now, too.

"Stay here." Derek unlocked the dead bolt and swung his gun behind his back. "I mean it this time."

"What?" Maisy stepped into the kitchen, closer to the opposite door. "What's happening?"

"My truck's back," Derek said. "I'm going to meet my little brother outside."

Maisy's breaths came short and quick as Derek left her in the cabin, pulling the door shut behind him. She accessed her cell phone's dial pad and put 911 on the screen, then hovered her thumb over the green button, ready to send the call.

Outside, a round of husky laughter echoed in the air.

She took a small step forward, listening intently.

"All right, man," Blaze said, his voice boisterous and friendly.

Maisy hurried for a look out the window.

Blaze spoke to the man in coveralls, a welcoming smile on his face.

Derek slunk around the large white work truck, taking photos of the license plate and through the window of the cab, then several of the man speaking with Blaze.

Maisy erased 911 from her dial pad and called the resort's lodge instead, eyes fixed on the men outside. She started as the silhouette of someone inside Derek's truck caught her eye. She'd temporarily forgotten the lawyer was coming to talk with her.

"Yes, hello," Maisy said to the woman answering her call. "I just saw a man in one of your trucks lurking along the roadside. Is he allowed to do that?" she asked, making her voice high and working up a deep southern accent. "He isn't some kind of voyeur, is he?"

"No, ma'am," the woman responded. "Our maintenance crew is out clearing ditches today. The rain has washed the storm drains full of leaves and mud, which has caused some minor flooding in a few areas. We wouldn't want those to freeze when the temperature drops again tonight. Ice on these roads can make travel nearly impossible. If you'd like, I can confirm the man's name and description, so you know he's where he should be and doing what he's supposed to be doing. Did you happen to notice the number on the truck?"

Maisy hesitated. As much as she'd like the confirmation, she hated to give away her location. Blaze was supposed to be an artist staying alone. She watched as he and Derek waved goodbye to the man then turned toward the cabin. If they were satisfied, she would be, too. "No, thank you," she said. "I can see it's fine. Goodbye."

The man in coveralls climbed back into his truck and drove away as the cabin door swung open. Derek arrived first. "That guy seemed legit. I took some pictures to check up on him and the truck, but you don't need to worry."

She smiled. "I won't. The lodge confirmed—"

"Hey," Blaze interrupted, crossing the

threshold with a willowy brunette. "We're back." His smile was triumphant, and Maisy found her smile widening in response. "Maisy Daniels. I would like you to meet Julia Struthers, the new lead prosecutor. Your second-biggest advocate."

Maisy warmed, knowing Blaze was her first.

Julia extended a hand to Maisy. Her dark hair fell in curtains against her cheeks and jaw, streaked with gray and grazing her shoulders. Her smart green eyes scanned Maisy warmly. A motherly smile curved her petal-pink lips.

"Thank you for doing this," Maisy said. "For taking up the torch. For coming here. It's very courageous of you."

"I'm no more courageous than the woman at this case's center," she said with a wry grin. "I've been following your sister's case from the beginning. Your love and devotion has been evident from the start. Not many people know this, but I left trial law for teaching because I'd become so exhausted by the number of people willing to walk away from justice if the right amount of money was offered."

Maisy tried to imagine taking money in exchange for dropping the charges against Natalie's killer. But she couldn't. How could anyone?

Julia's expression turned sad and knowing.

"You've probably noticed no one from your friend Aaron's family plans to testify."

A spark of surprise zipped through her. She hadn't given him much thought in the past few months, but she'd assumed his family was pursuing Luciano as actively as she was. She'd expected to see them at the trial. "They dropped their charges?"

Julia nodded. "They can still be subpoenaed, compelled to provide testimony, but I don't plan to do that. They've made their position clear. They're at peace with the loss they can't change. They aren't comfortable dredging up their most horrible memories. Forcing them to take the stand could wind up hurting our case. It's better to focus on what we have working for us."

"You think Aaron's parents were bribed?" Maisy asked.

"Or threatened," Julia said. "Either way, I won't press the matter. They've been through too much already. Just like you. But if you're still willing to testify, I will stick by you every step of the way."

Maisy pulled in a fortifying breath and released it with a smile. She would do anything to see Luciano never hurt anyone else again. "Let's get started."

Chapter Eighteen

Blaze walked Derek to his truck after a late dinner. They'd made chicken noodle soup from cans and baked rolls in the oven. It wasn't a fancy meal, but it was warm, comforting and cozy, filling the cabin with the rich, buttery scents of home. A perfect ending to a successful day. Maisy had connected with Julia in a real and trusting way during her visit, and Maisy's testimony had been recorded, in case it wasn't safe for her to attend the trial.

Blaze had taken Julia back to the coffee shop where they'd met, then returned in time to help with dinner. Maisy had been in good spirits, though she'd eaten far less than he thought she should. Now, it was time for Derek to go home temporarily. He'd made the same short escape the day before, leaving to care for his horses and get some sleep before returning to keep watch while Blaze tried to rest a few hours before dawn.

"I'll be back by midnight," Derek said, squinting as the snow fell over them.

Blaze rubbed tired eyes and struggled to suppress a yawn. "Take your time. If I haven't told you lately, I appreciate what you've been doing here. So does Maisy."

"What are brothers for?" Derek grinned. He clapped Blaze on the back, then pointed his eyes at the cabin. "Keep an eye on her tonight. She was sick all day and lied about it."

"You noticed that, too, huh?" Blaze followed his brother's gaze to the flicker of light from the television inside the front window.

"Yep. I'm guessing she doesn't want to worry you."

"Well, it's too late for that," Blaze said. "All I do is worry."

"Three more days," Derek said. "You're almost there. With a little luck, Julia will convince Judge Wise to accept the recording as evidence tonight, or the other attorney will agree to a livestream during the trial."

Blaze forced a smile, but they both knew Maisy's luck wasn't that good. "Maybe," he conceded. "I'm going to give her doctor a call when I go back inside. That should help put some of my anxiety to rest. Maisy will protest, until I say I'm worried about the baby, then she won't fight me on it. There's nothing she won't do for her."

"Her?" Derek's brows tented. "A little girl? Are you sure?"

Blaze beamed, unable to stop himself. "I wanted to let her tell you, but these last few days have been nuts."

"A girl?"

Blaze nodded. "Yeah. She's going to make a great mom."

Derek pulled Blaze into a hug. "And you're going to make a great dad. You already have all those awful jokes."

"Shut up." Blaze shoved him toward the open truck door. "Go home. Drive safely. Come back rested." He shook his head as he climbed the steps to the cabin's small porch, then watched as the truck's taillights faded slowly into the distance.

Every minute that passed without a crisis was a cherished moment closer to the end of the chaos. A moment closer to his new beginning with Maisy.

He stomped snow from his shoes before slipping inside.

Maisy smiled at him from the kitchen. She leaned against the countertop, a glass of water in one hand. Uncertainty colored her cheeks, and as he toed off his boots and drew closer, a line of sweat became evident over her brow. "Everything okay?"

"I was going to ask you the same thing," Blaze said. He pressed the back of his hand to her forehead, then pulled her into a hug. "You aren't fevered, but you're clammy. Does that mean you're trying to hide nausea or contractions?"

She stepped away with a grimace, wrapping both arms around her middle. "I just need to lie down. It's been a big day, and I ate too much at dinner."

"You barely ate anything at dinner," he said. "And you've looked like this since we left the courthouse yesterday. Tell me what's going on."

Maisy pressed her eyes and lips shut briefly before peeling weary hazel eyes open once more. "Fine. I don't feel well. I'm nauseous and tense. My stomach's been upset more often than it hasn't, and my back aches almost non-stop."

Fear flattened Blaze's heart. He struggled to maintain his warm smile while fishing his phone from his pocket. "Come here." Her pulled her against him, rubbing his palm against her back as she snuggled close.

Maisy pressed her cheek to his chest. "I can't shake the nausea. I've been reading online all day about it, and I think it's normal, especially under stress, but I can't seem to get rid of it. I've tried everything."

Blaze kissed the top of her head. "Why don't I call Dr. Nazir? She'll know if it's anything to worry about, and what we should do either way."

Maisy nodded, releasing him slowly, then let him lead her to the couch.

"Give me just a minute." He scrolled to the doctor's number, saved in his phone, then called, switching on the speaker function so Maisy could listen in and take part.

Dr. Nazir was pleasant, but concerned. She worried about Maisy's hydration, and suggested Blaze get her a sports drink to help the cause. She also recommended a safe, over-the-counter pill for the nausea.

Maisy was visibly relieved when the call disconnected. "I'm going to be okay," she said wistfully.

"Sounds like it," Blaze agreed.

Still, her skin was pale and dewy from a sheen of sweat. "It's the stress," she insisted, dragging a forearm across her brow.

Blaze propped Maisy's feet on a pair of throw pillows, then delivered a cold, wet washcloth for her forehead. "We'll visit Dr. Nazir's office first thing tomorrow morning," he said.

"For tonight, rest and hydration." He knelt on the floor before her, concern tightening his limbs and gut. "I'm going to run to the general store before it closes and pick up the medication she recommended for nausea." He checked his watch. "I can make it if I leave now, and bring you back something to help with hydration, too."

He had another thirty minutes before the store closed, but he only needed seven to get there, and five to gather the items on his list. Resort roads would be empty this time of day in the off-season, making it possible to double the posted speed limit.

She reached for him, curling her small hand around his much larger one. "Thank you for taking care of me." A small tear hung in the corner of her eye.

Blaze caught the droplet with the pad of his thumb and brushed her hair away from flushed cheeks. "I will always take care of you."

Her returning smile pinched his heart, and he sent up a silent prayer that she would feel better soon. That she would rest, and that the doctor would tell them she and their baby were perfect after seeing her tomorrow morning.

Blaze had been a soldier, had been shot at in foreign lands and had been endangered regularly since becoming a homicide detective, but he'd never been afraid like he was now. He lifted her hand to his lips and pressed a kiss against her knuckles, then another to her forehead, sneakily checking for signs of a fever. Thankfully, she was cool.

"If you're going to be at the store," she said, looking shyly up at him, "see if they have those little oyster crackers? And more herbal tea? I've gone through most of our stash."

"You've got it," Blaze said. He collected her cell phone from the kitchen counter and placed it on the coffee table in front of her, wishing he had another Taser to offer. "The cabin's locked up tight, but call me if you hear or see anything that makes you uncomfortable. Better to sound a false alarm than miss an opportunity for help." He hesitated, torn between what he knew she needed right now, and the help she might need if he left. The pallor of her skin and faint grimace of discomfort she tried to hide made the former impossible to ignore. "I'll be back as quickly as possible."

He kissed her gently, then dashed outside, carefully locking the door behind him.

The drive down the mountain was fraught with unexpected clusters of actual deer in the headlights, but Blaze made it to the general store in under ten minutes, despite the wildlife roadblocks. He parked near the door in an otherwise empty parking lot, then hustled inside with his mental shopping list.

The aisles were void of people, but well stocked, much like before. And he found everything he needed in minutes. His arms were loaded when he reached the counter. "How much for the flowers?" he asked, righting his purchases on the counter. He swung a finger toward the bouquet of miniature pink, orange and cream roses on display.

The older man behind the register lifted a pair of glasses from his pocket and set them on his nose. "I remember you," he said, passing the bouquet in question to Blaze. "You were here a few days ago with your wife, right?"

"No, sir," Blaze said, hating the fact Derek had been right. This man remembered them, and that could be very dangerous for Maisy and their baby.

"Yes, yes." The man smiled. "Maybe she wasn't your wife. I don't know, but she was lovely. Brown hair, hazel eyes. Pregnant," he reminded Blaze, mimicking the shape of her bump with his hands. "The flowers are on me," he said. "How's she holding up?" He pulled the crackers and sports drinks across the counter to scan them. "I remember these days." He laughed. "My Margaret ate her weight in crackers when she was pregnant with our sons. What are you having? A boy or a girl?"

Blaze pushed the other items closer for the man to ring them up. His mind reeled over how to answer. Was there a way to ask him not to let anyone know they were there, without telling him why it was so important their whereabouts stay concealed? Blaze could show his badge, mention the trial that was on every newscast. But was this man trustworthy?

Would knowing put him in danger?

"Twenty-five twelve," the clerk said, dropping the last item in the bag. "I didn't mean to pry," he apologized, still smiling. "I get a little bored in the off-season. It's lonely. I talk too much."

Exactly what Blaze was afraid of.

"You can let her know her friend's arrangement made it to the funeral on time, just as promised." He shrugged. "Like I said, I've got a lot of extra time, and she looked so heartbroken when she placed the order. I wanted to be sure the flowers made it to their destination safely, so I gave the place a call."

"Funeral?" Blaze asked, passing a pair of twenties across the counter. "She asked you to send flowers to a funeral?"

"Sure." The man tapped the cash register, and the drawer popped open. "We're part of the National Flower Distribution Network." He handed Blaze his change and receipt, then pointed to a pink flyer on the window.

"Can you tell me exactly where those flowers went?" Blaze asked, stuffing the wallet back into his pocket and gathering the bags with Maisy's bouquet. Not that he needed confirmation to know they'd been for Clara. Of course she'd want to send her condolences. Why hadn't he thought to handle this for her? She could've made the selection, and Derek could've handled the delivery. He could only hope she'd been wise enough to pay in cash and not include a card.

The man presented a completed order form. Fake information in the sender section. Good. Delivery details were as expected. Clara's memorial service in North Jackson.

"Did she include a card with the order?" he asked, feeling slightly more comfortable with the situation.

"She didn't specify, so I wrote 'warmest thoughts and prayers.' That's the standard for funeral arrangements."

"Did she pay cash? Or sign the card?"

"Yes to both, though she only signed with her initials."

Blaze's grip tightened on the flowers and packages. That was half of what he'd wanted to hear. "May I see the cards you include in these matters?" He watched raptly as the man fished one from a pile behind him. Blaze begged silently that the small white square be marked with the national chain name only.

"There." He passed a blank card to Blaze with a smile.

Brandy Falls Ski Resort was embossed in golden font across the top.

MAISY SHUFFLED AROUND the living room, nausea pushed aside by a powerful, teeth-gritting contraction. Her nerves were wholly and completely shot, and she was beginning to panic. It was the first time she'd been alone since leaving her safe house behind. Before that, it had been months. Now, the trial was less than seventy-two hours away, people associated with it were dropping like flies and her body was reacting just as extremely as her mind.

Every sound in the forest sent fresh waves of terror down her spine as she puffed through another false contraction. She imagined shooters in the trees, taking aim through the windows. Killers lurking in the shadows along the exterior wall, just out of sight and slowly prying open the cabin windows and doors.

The sound of an engine outside sent her hurrying to the front window, eager to see Blaze's strong, comforting smile.

The big ski resort truck was back, parked along the road's edge again.

She collected her phone from the coffee table and hesitated. Call the lodge to confirm the worker was back? Tending to gutters after dark? Or call Blaze to tell him she was in pain and scaring herself silly?

Her phone rang before she could decide, and Blaze's face appeared on the screen. She smiled in relief. Sometimes she was sure they shared a cosmic connection. At the moment she was intensely thankful for it. "Hello?"

"Maisy?" Blaze's voice was a mashup of tension and fear. "Did you send flowers to Clara's funeral?"

"Yes," she said, attention glued to the man in coveralls climbing out of the truck. "It was impulsive, but I was careful. I was going to tell you right after I did it, but I got distracted. Listen," she rattled on, unable to pause or catch her breath. "The man is back to clean the gutters, and I'm kind of freaking out about it."

Blaze swore. "Check the door locks, and turn the lights out. Just to be safe. I'm in my truck now."

Across the phone line, an engine revved to life. Maisy hit the light switch, then tucked her feet into sneakers, kept on standby near the rear door. "I didn't sign my name to the card. How'd you find out about it, and why does it matter? Also, please tell me I'm overreacting about this ditch cleaner."

Blaze's truck engine roared across the line. "You used your initials. And the card was embossed with the ski resort's logo. Go into your room and lock the door. I'll talk to the guy when I get there."

Maisy's gaze darted through the dark cabin. There was nowhere to hide, and a hollow interior door with a cheap knob lock couldn't protect her.

Outside, the man in coveralls headed up her walk, a shovel swung onto his shoulder like a baseball bat. "He's coming," she whispered, stumbling backward against the rear door. Moonlight glinted on the handgun at his hip as he reached the small front porch.

He knocked. Then tried the knob.

There was only one thing left for Maisy to do.

Run.

Chapter Nineteen

Maisy stepped into the biting cold, heart racing and instantly regretful that she hadn't grabbed a coat when she put on her sneakers.

"Are you there?" Blaze barked. "Is he in the house? Are you hidden?"

The sudden crash of their cabin's door bursting open set her feet in motion. She choked back a scream as fear propelled her through the snowy woods. "He's inside. I think he broke down the door. I'm outside. I'm running. Blaze, hurry!"

Icy winds burned her skin, slicing easily through her thin cotton pajamas. She pulled hair from her eyes as she muddled forward, over tree roots and mud. Her steps were uneven, thrown off by her too-high center of gravity. She slid on wet leaves and patches of icy earth, tossing her forward and nearly onto her knees. Her heartbeat pounded in her ears as she raced into the night, desperately adding space between herself and the killer.

"You can't hide!" An angry male voice echoed behind her. "I know you're out here, and you're never going to make it back inside alive."

"He's outside now. He knows I'm out here," Maisy cried into the phone.

"Stay put. I'm two minutes out," Blaze growled.

Maisy couldn't stop, couldn't risk being caught, couldn't risk her baby's life.

She dared a look behind her and felt her rioting heart collapse.

The man had a spotlight.

Her toe clipped something hard and immobile on the forest floor, pitching her forward as she turned her attention back around. She crashed sideways into a large evergreen and involuntarily yipped in pain. Her cell phone popped loose from her grip and collided with the snowy ground. Rough bark tore the tender skin of her arm, aching and stinging as she bit back another cry. Heavy breaths puffed from her lips in smoky white clouds as she edged around the tree, pressing her back to the wood, listening for signs of his nearness.

Maisy's eyes blurred with unshed tears as

her footprints came into view on the snowy ground, marking a path to her hiding spot.

Bang! The blast of a gun split the night, ringing her ears and scattering birds from the treetops.

Bang!

Bark burst into bits at her side.

Maisy darted into the thickest part of the forest, praying the limbs of heavy pines and multitude of trunks would disguise her plight.

A third shot rang out, exploding divots of earth over the snow several yards away.

She locked her jaw against another scream, unwilling to disclose her position and knowing the shooter would soon catch her anyway. Her stomach twisted with nausea, and a contraction gripped her middle hard enough to double her over.

"You can't hide," the voice bellowed. "You've left me a path, and you can't run forever in your condition."

Maisy forced her trembling legs to move, forcing her fear into a mental lockbox. She had to live. Had to protect her baby. *And Blaze will be here soon*, she reminded herself.

She just had to stay alive long enough to be rescued.

Maisy ducked beneath the heaviest limbs, crouching as she hurried through a thick blanket of fallen pine needles, making her footsteps invisible.

Something moved in the distance, and Maisy yelped.

A deer ran through the forest, and another gunshot went off.

The little she'd eaten made a reappearance at her feet, spilled freely at the thought of the poor deer's possible fate. Her throat burned, and her teeth began to chatter as she pitched herself forward once more. Carried on wobbly knees and frozen legs across the pine needles, refusing to look back. Unwilling to see if the deer had made it, or if the poor thing had become another casualty in the war she had started.

The cadence of steady footfalls rose through the night, close enough now to be heard. Close enough for the next shot not to miss.

And Maisy had nowhere left to hide. The trees ended a few yards ahead, opening broadly to a large snow-covered field.

She scooted around the massive trunk, then backed herself into a gaping hollow at its core, trying to make herself as small as possible.

The broad beam of her hunter's spotlight flashed into view across the forest floor. Snow crunched under his feet as he stopped only a few feet from the tree.

Maisy's breaths raked loudly through her ears, each exhale a smoke signal to her hiding spot.

The next contraction hit like a sledgehammer, buckling her knees where she stood.

And a trickle of something warm and wet rolled down her thigh.

"Maisy!" Blaze's voice echoed in the trees, bringing a flood of hot tears to her eyes.

Outside her narrow hiding place, the spotlight vanished, and her hunter's footfalls moved away.

She melted into the tree with short-lived relief.

Then the gunshots began.

"Police!" Blaze called between blasts, his voice low and bursting with authority. "You are under arrest. Put down your weapon. Now!"

Another shot sounded, and Maisy's ears rang anew. Choked by fear and a constricting chest, the world began to darken around her.

A steady beating erupted, and the trees began to sway.

The pain of a fresh contraction broke over her, hitting like a punch in the spine and forcing her legs out from under her. She slid down the rotted tree, its frozen bark pulling up the back of her shirt and breaking the skin as she fell. Her numb and frozen hands reached for the ground to soften her landing in the pine needles and snow.

A tortured scream ripped through her as the next contraction followed in the wake of the last. Moist heat warmed her trembling thighs as she rolled onto her back on the frozen ground. Above her, the treetops undulated wildly, and the beating grew impossibly loud.

Her breaths came short and shallow. She pinched her eyes closed against the pain.

"Maisy! Maisy!"

She peeled her eyes open, unsure how long they'd been closed. The unequivocal ache at her core nearly too much to bear.

A blinding light hovered in the sky, and she shut her eyes once more.

"She's here!" Blaze called, then his arms were around her. "Stay with me," he pleaded, but her frozen lips couldn't form a response.

Her body writhed with the next contraction, and she was sure she'd die.

"It's okay," Blaze demanded. "I'm here. We've got you."

Sleet pelted her face as the silhouettes of strangers surrounded her, aiding Blaze as he carried her into the light. Toward the beating sound.

Onto a helicopter and into the air.

Chapter Twenty

Blaze watched helplessly as the medical staff at West Liberty United Hospital rushed Maisy down the hall ahead of him on a gurney. A flood of panic and adrenaline tunneled his vision and rung his ears. Scents of bleach and bandages stung his nose and throat as he jogged the corridor toward the maternity ward.

He owed everything to the chopper pilot and crew who'd landed in the snowy field, charged with the capture and arrest of Luciano's hit man. They'd easily changed missions when they found Blaze with her, unconscious, in his arms. The helicopter had flown Maisy to the hospital in less time than it would've taken Blaze to carry her out of the woods and meet the arriving ambulance. The ambulance would've taken another twenty minutes to drive her off the mountain.

The pilot had radioed ahead to alert the hospital, and the hospital had contacted Dr. Nazir.

Now, Blaze could only hope Maisy and their daughter would be okay.

"What can you tell us about her condition?" an older woman in blue scrubs asked over her shoulder.

"She's been nauseous all day," Blaze said. "She's had intermittent contractions for much longer. More than a week, at least." The words poured from him, almost faster than he could speak them. "She was in the woods at least thirty minutes without a coat before I found her. She was hiding. I apprehended the shooter," he rambled, "then I couldn't find her. She's been in and out of consciousness."

"Shooter?" a second, younger nurse, helping pilot the gurney, asked.

"She's a witness in a trial this week," Blaze answered, slowing with the group as a broad set of doors marked Obstetrics swung open before them.

The older woman glanced at him once more, expression firm. "This is Maisy Daniels? The woman from the news?"

"Yes, ma'am."

She gave Maisy's slack face a long look, then pushed Maisy's medical chariot into the ward. "How far apart are the contractions now?"

Blaze's mind faltered and scrambled. "I don't know." So much had happened so quickly, he hadn't thought to keep track. He'd only worried that he'd been too late to save her. "Not long. A few minutes."

"Put her in a delivery room," the older woman told the younger one. "I'll perform an exam and call anesthesiology to get someone on standby for an epidural."

"She's not due for five weeks," Blaze said, a bead of fresh panic welling in his heart.

Dr. Nazir had given him one job. He was supposed to keep Maisy safe, rested and relaxed. Because she needed to maintain her pregnancy as long as possible. It'd only been days since he'd promised to do those things no matter what, and he'd failed.

And Maisy would pay the price.

The nurses parted ways at the next intersection of hallways.

Blaze stuck close to the younger woman piloting Maisy's gurney, buzzing past arrows with Labor and Delivery written across their centers, while the older woman jogged toward a massive nurses' station.

Maisy's head rolled over her shoulder, her arms limp at her sides.

She'd been eerily white when Blaze had found her. Her cheeks red and lips blue. Her thin canvas sneakers and cotton pajamas were soaked with melted snow.

The nurse drove Maisy's gurney into room 427 and parked it beside a waiting bed, then clamped the brakes.

The older woman returned, rushing past Blaze where he'd stalled just inside the doorway. "Let's get her out of those wet things and into a gown. I brought a set of heated blankets. Ready?"

Maisy's eyes fluttered open as the nurses changed her, then hauled her onto the bed and covered her. "It's too soon. You have to stop the contractions," she pleaded weakly. "She can't come yet."

The following scream and grimace on her pale, twisted face said differently.

The baby was definitely coming.

The nurses moved in a perfectly choreographed dance. Setting Maisy's IV and connecting her body to a barrage of nearby monitors within minutes.

The older nurse pulled a pair of gloves from a bin on the wall and pressed her hands into them. "I'm going to take a look now and see what's going on. Okay, Maisy?"

Maisy agreed, and the older woman moved to the foot of the bed.

Blaze's limbs seemed to lock in place. "Don't we have to wait for the doctor?"

The nurse started at the sound of his voice,

as if she'd just taken notice of him. Her gaze slid pointedly to the badge hanging from the chain around his neck. "You can go now, Detective. We'll take it from here."

"What?" he stammered, confusion clouding his brain. "I can't stay?" he asked, his normally confident voice no more than a hoarse whisper.

The woman's expression swung hard from shock to distaste. "I'm afraid not. There's a chair just outside the door if you need to guard your witness."

"No!" Maisy groaned the word around another contraction.

"She's not my witness," he said, heart aching, fcet rooted. She might've started that way, in what felt like another lifetime, but now, he realized, now, she was his life.

Maisy's thin arms clung to her middle, her eyes and jaw clamped tight. "He's the father."

A banner of pride swept through Blaze's chest at the words, and the weight of their significance.

The nurse's eyes widened. "I'm so sorry. I didn't realize. Given the situation..."

"It's fine," he said, moving slowly forward. "But is she okay?"

The nurse nodded to the chair beside the bed. "Come. I'll see if it's time we talk about that epidural."

Blaze moved to the head of Maisy's bed and reached for her hand. Her fingers were cold, and images of the darkened forest rushed back to his mind. He'd nearly been shot by her assailant before eventually shooting him instead. It had taken all of Blaze's restraint, and the knowledge that Maisy was missing, to stop him from emptying his entire clip into the lunatic. Instead, he'd kicked the man's gun away, checked his pulse then cuffed him to a tree as the sirens of emergency vehicles became audible in the distance.

With a little karma, the hit man would wind up on the same cell block as Luciano.

By the time Blaze found Maisy, the cavalry had arrived, thanks to Sergeant Maxwell. He'd identified the leak in their system earlier that morning. Luciano was blackmailing a guard at the jail. His image was visible, reflected in the glass of the police station door he'd left ajar for the intruder who'd attacked Maisy in the ladies' room. Fortunately, the man spilled everything while under interrogation. And he'd agreed to testify in exchange for leniency.

When word made it to Lucas that the shooter was headed to the ski resort, he told Maxwell that Blaze was hiding Maisy there. A team and chopper were dispatched, along with local police.

Unfortunately, Blaze hadn't been there to protect her when she'd needed him most.

Whatever happened to her and their baby now would forever be on him.

Maisy screamed again, thrusting her head and shoulders forward. Pain etched hard lines over her delicate features as her entire body seemed to tighten.

"No time for an epidural," the nurse said brightly. "The baby is coming."

TWO DAYS LATER, Maisy kissed her daughter's tiny, perfect fingers while slowly memorizing every feature and contour of her small face. From her dad's gray eyes to her precious rosebud lips, she was more than Maisy had ever dreamed of.

Born more than a month early, Natalie Clara Winchester was a late-term preemie. She might've weighed in at just over five pounds, but she more than earned her name every day. Because just like Natalie and Clara, Maisy's little princess was a fighter.

"I'll be back soon," Maisy promised, raising her daughter's delicate hand to her lips for a kiss. "I wouldn't leave if I didn't have to, but there's something very important I need to do. Until then, the nurses will take good care of you."

Blaze wrapped a strong arm around Maisy's

middle and pulled her against him, cool gray eyes fixed on their perfect daughter. "I'm so proud of you both." He kissed Maisy's head, then rested his cheek against the crown of her head for a long moment. "The two toughest ladies I know."

"Yeah? Then why do I feel like crying, or cuffing myself to her bed?" Maisy asked, laughing awkwardly at the ridiculous truth. "I've never been farther than a few doors down the hall from her. It feels like ripping off one of my limbs," she said, emotions clogging her throat at the thought of telling her baby good-bye.

"She'll be fine," Blaze whispered. "She'll rest and grow and dream of her mama until you return."

Maisy smiled, enjoying that thought and hoping it was true. "I love her so much. I didn't know I could love someone so completely," she whispered, gazing at their infant in the NICU, a precautionary move, given her size and precarious beginning.

"I did," Blaze said, lifting her face to his for a chaste kiss.

Maisy's hands rose to his chest, fingertips landing gently on the smooth fabric of his tie. "Thank you for always being so kind and loving and patient with me." He was the embodiment of all her favorite qualities in a human, a partner and a friend. And even after a few short days, she had no doubt he was going to make the world's best father.

Blaze chuckled low in his throat. "Maybe you just bring out the best in me." He kissed her forehead. Her closed eyelids, the tip of her nose. "Are you ready?"

"Not even close," she said, lacing her fingers with his as they walked away from the NICU, casting more than a few backward glances at their little girl.

"You've got this," Blaze promised. "And I've got you."

The most comforting words she'd ever heard.

Maisy concentrated on her breathing and the feel of his hand in hers as she followed him out of the hospital.

Then into the courtroom.

Epilogue

Maisy rolled onto her side in bed, instinctively reaching for Blaze. She hadn't slept alone since leaving the hospital two months ago, and she loved having him so near. Her fingertips slid over the cool, rumpled sheets. Her sleepy eyes peeled open when her hands came up empty.

Blaze's side of the bed had clearly been slept in, but he wasn't there.

She rose onto her elbows, searching for signs of him in the dark, but found none.

The baby monitor on the nightstand was silent, unplugged or powered off, and an icy finger of fear slithered up her spine. Unwelcomed memories skittered through her mind. Memories where she and her baby were in danger.

Memories, she reminded herself, *nothing more.* And that wasn't her life any longer.

She climbed out of bed with her chin held high, then wrapped herself in the fuzzy robe on the bedpost. She'd accomplished her goal, as promised. With Blaze's help, she'd been able to give testimony in court against Luciano that helped the jury find him guilty. Now, he would live out his days in Kentucky's supermax prison.

Which meant that Maisy was safe.

Better than safe, she thought, tying the belt on her robe. She was loved and happy, healthy and pampered.

Blaze had invited her and Natalie to stay with him until Maisy could find a job and save enough money to move out. She'd eagerly agreed. Her life at the safe house was over, but her old life, the one from before Luciano, was packed into a storage unit. Her apartment long ago rented to someone else.

Now, she was a single, homeless, unemployed mother of an infant.

Thankfully, Blaze's invitation was open-ended, and he told her daily how much he loved having her and Natalie with him. He asked her not to rush into looking for work, not that she'd worked in forever, and when she had, the jobs were never especially wonderful. She'd put her office administration degree to work with paying bills as her singular goal. Now, Blaze told her not to settle. To only choose something she loved. Until then, he encouraged her to preserve every moment she had with their infant daughter for as long as possible, and he'd vowed to help however he could. True to his words and nature, he did more than his share of everything, from cooking and cleaning to late-night feedings and diaper changes. And he seemed to enjoy it all.

Maisy and Natalie certainly enjoyed him. His humor, love and company. She couldn't imagine leaving, so she tried not to think about it. The notion left her empty and cold.

Natalie deserved to spend every minute she could in her daddy's adoring arms. A lifetime of him looking at her as if she might walk on water, if she could walk at all, should ensure that no man would ever get away with mistreating her.

Outside the bedroom, moonlight streamed through gauzy white curtains, painting silver lines across the wide wooden floorboards. She tiptoed softly toward the little nursery, listening carefully for sounds he was there.

The low tenor of his voice sent gooseflesh down her arms, and she strained to make out the words.

Natalie cooed, and Blaze chuckled.

Maisy smiled, falling deeper in love with the both of them as she drifted closer. Eager for a peek at their late-night fun.

"Knock, knock," she whispered, pushing the door slowly open.

The space that had once been little more than a storage room had become the most enchanting nursery Maisy had ever seen. Blaze had worked on it, day by day, until it was perfect. The walls were a faint pink, with accents in ivory and cream. A flowing white curtain draped over the single window, held back by a long velvet tie. A floppy white elephant, wearing a tutu and tiara, sat on Blaze's mother's rocking chair in the corner, a hot-pink shag rug beneath it. Twinkle lights lined the ceiling, and a massive growth chart, made by Derek from an old barn beam, was anchored to the wall. Natalie's toy box brimmed with things she wouldn't be old enough to play with for a year and stood outside a refinished wardrobe filled with enough dresses to clothe a dozen little girls, and accessories to go with every one.

Natalie's little booties came into view, busy as always, narrow legs kicking away her long pink nightgown. Dainty fists waved above her head. A tiny bundle of energy. Always in motion. Going nowhere, but tickled to death about it.

Maisy's heart leaped and her smile doubled at the sight of her. "What are you doing?" she asked, slipping into the dimly lit room. Her daughter's perfect cherub face and cool gray eyes turned to look up at her.

She reached for her baby, raising her lovingly to her chest before turning to search the space for Blaze. She stopped short as a glint of light drew her eyes to the mobile of happy clouds dancing above the crib.

A diamond ring dangled from the white satin ribbon tied to a cloud.

Her breath caught at the sight of it.

"Maisy?" Blaze's voice turned her toward the shadows, where he'd apparently slipped away for a surprise appearance.

She snuggled Natalie closer, tears of joy forming in her eyes. "I woke up and you weren't there," she said, trying to sound more calm than she suddenly felt. "I thought I'd find you here."

Blaze moved in closer, eyes dancing with delight. "Natalie and I have some serious heart-to-heart talks this time of night."

Maisy laughed. "Oh yeah?" She commanded herself not to look at the ring. Maybe he didn't know she'd seen it. Maybe she wasn't meant to. "What do you talk about?"

Blaze kissed his daughter on her forehead, then he reached for the ring from the mobile, casting a mischievous look over one shoulder. "Sometimes NASCAR. Sometimes the Nasdaq." His smile widened as he stepped back, ring in hand. "Mostly you, and how much we love you."

"Oh yeah?" Maisy's cheeks heated, and her body warmed with his words. Blaze had never left her wondering how much he cared about her, but the ring was more than she'd dared to hope for. She'd wanted to believe that, someday, if things went well for a year or so, he might want to take another step with her. After she was on her feet again, and they'd dated long enough for him to be sure that she was what he wanted. Forever. The way she'd known the same about him since practically the moment they'd met.

Blaze pinched the classic solitaire's band between his thumb and forefinger. Then he lowered onto his knee and said the most perfect two words she'd ever heard him say. "Marry me?"

And Maisy said, "Yes."

* * * * *

*Look for more books in
Julie Anne Lindsey's
Heartland Heroes miniseries
later this year.*

*And don't miss the previous book
in the series,*
SVU Surveillance, *available now wherever
Harlequin Intrigue books are sold!*

Get 4 FREE REWARDS!

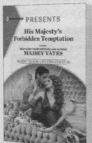

We'll send you 2 FREE Books plus 2 FREE Mystery Gifts.

Harlequin Presents books feature the glamorous lives of royals and billionaires in a world of exotic locations, where passion knows no bounds.

FREE Value Over $20

Get 4 FREE REWARDS!

We'll send you 2 FREE Books plus 2 FREE Mystery Gifts.

FREE Value Over **$20**

Both the **Romance** and **Suspense** collections feature compelling novels written by many of today's bestselling authors.

YES! Please send me 2 FREE novels from the Essential Romance or Essential Suspense Collection and my 2 FREE gifts (gifts are worth about $10 retail). After receiving them, if I don't wish to receive any more books, I can return the shipping statement marked "cancel." If I don't cancel, I will receive 4 brand-new novels every month and be billed just $7.24 each in the U.S. or $7.49 each in Canada. That's a savings of up to 28% off the cover price. It's quite a bargain! Shipping and handling is just 50¢ per book in the U.S. and $1.25 per book in Canada.* I understand that accepting the 2 free books and gifts places me under no obligation to buy anything. I can always return a shipment and cancel at any time. The free books and gifts are mine to keep no matter what I decide.

Choose one: ☐ **Essential Romance**
(194/394 MDN GQ6M)

☐ **Essential Suspense**
(191/391 MDN GQ6M)

Name (please print)

Address   Apt. #

City   State/Province   Zip/Postal Code

Email: Please check this box ☐ if you would like to receive newsletters and promotional emails from Harlequin Enterprises ULC and its affiliates. You can unsubscribe anytime.

Mail to the **Harlequin Reader Service:**
IN U.S.A.: P.O. Box 1341, Buffalo, NY 14240-8531
IN CANADA: P.O. Box 603, Fort Erie, Ontario L2A 5X3

Want to try 2 free books from another series? Call 1-800-873-8635 or visit www.ReaderService.com.

*Terms and prices subject to change without notice. Prices do not include sales taxes, which will be charged (if applicable) based on your state or country of residence. Canadian residents will be charged applicable taxes. Offer not valid in Quebec. This offer is limited to one order per household. Books received may not be as shown. Not valid for current subscribers to the Essential Romance or Essential Suspense Collection. All orders subject to approval. Credit or debit balances in a customer's account(s) may be offset by any other outstanding balance owed by or to the customer. Please allow 4 to 6 weeks for delivery. Offer available while quantities last.

Your Privacy—Your information is being collected by Harlequin Enterprises ULC, operating as Harlequin Reader Service. For a complete summary of the information we collect, how we use this information and to whom it is disclosed, please visit our privacy notice located at corporate.harlequin.com/privacy-notice. From time to time we may also exchange your personal information with reputable third parties. If you wish to opt out of this sharing of your personal information, please visit readerservice.com/consumerchoice or call 1-800-873-8635. **Notice to California Residents**—Under California law, you have specific rights to control and access your data. For more information on these rights and how to exercise them, visit corporate.harlequin.com/california-privacy.

STRS21R